CLANCY'S
Glorious Fourth

CLANCY'S
Glorious Fourth

Written and illustrated by JANE FLORY

HOUGHTON MIFFLIN COMPANY

The Riverside Press Cambridge

Also by
JANE FLORY
Peddler's Summer
A Tune for the Towpath
One Hundred and Eight Bells

U. S. **1548167**

*For
the girls,
who encourage and criticize
and pose and type.*

CLANCY'S
Glorious Fourth

THE early morning sun came in through the bedroom window and hit Clancy Chapman right smack in the eye. He stirred and yawned and gradually came awake. He knew he felt good, but he couldn't think exactly why. It was Friday, he knew, and the sun was shining — that was always a good sign — but what was so special about this day? He sat straight up in bed as he remembered.

It was Friday, the tenth of June — the last day of school! Wide awake now, Clancy jumped out of his tumbled bed and hurried to the window. It was still quite early. No one else in the house was stirring yet. And no one in any of the neighboring houses was up yet either, from the looks of it.

His big black cat, Jelly, came across the lawn with something in his mouth. Clancy knew it was Jelly's morning mouse, the one he always laid neatly at the back doorstep next to the milk bottles.

It was a beautiful morning. The birds were singing their heads off in the trees all around the Chapman yard. He could see the platform and ladder of the tree house high in the biggest tree of all. Later in the summer when the tree was in full leaf the tree house would be a wonderful secret hideout, completely hidden from the ground.

He could feel the excitement rise in him as he thought of all the summer days ahead — days for bike-riding and fishing, club meetings in the tree, and long lazy days of doing nothing at all.

His school clothes would be put away, and, except for Sunday, he wouldn't have to wear shoes again until school started in the fall. He wiggled his bare toes and stretched with pleasure.

Barn swallows were nesting again in the eaves of the carriage house, he noticed. They swooped in great swinging circles around the weathervane on the roof. Clancy wished briefly that the carriage house held a horse and buggy instead of their shiny automobile. But horses were getting scarce, even in a little town like Mapleton. The milkman drove one, of course, and the iceman, and some of the farmers outside of town. Mapleton was up to date, though, and most of the townspeople, including his father, drove cars. After all, it was 1922, and times were changing fast. Clancy enjoyed the car, but longed for a horse, too. He sighed and then brightened as he looked over at the house next door. The screen door slammed, and Dodie Haines, his worst enemy in the whole world, came out to get the milk. Clancy leaned farther out the window.

"Watch out you don't sour it, Dodie," he shouted, forgetting that his mother and father might still be sleeping. Dodie turned, and squinting against the sun, stuck out her tongue in his direction. Then she grabbed up the milk and flounced angrily into the house.

Pleased at having started Dodie's day off wrong, Clancy decided to get dressed. In a few minutes he was in the kitchen, noisily banging the icebox door, clattering pans, knocking over cereal boxes, whistling off key.

Jelly was waiting at the back door, meowing to come in. As Clancy unlatched the screen, Jelly laid his morning mouse on the doorstep and pushed his way in through the door. He hunted all night for fun, but hurried in impatiently the first thing in the morning to be fed in the Chapman kitchen.

Clancy sang as he poured out Jelly's saucer of milk. When his parents came down to breakfast, he was still singing.

"Hooray, hooray, this is the la-ast day!

Hooray, hooray — "

His mother asked curiously, "I always thought you liked school, Clancy. Why so anxious to have it over with?"

Clancy rumpled his unruly red hair that was so

3

like his father's and scratched his freckled nose.

"I do like school, usually. But this year — I don't know, seems as if I've been *in* trouble more than I've been out. Miss Cartwright made me write a hundred million sentences on the board for one thing or another."

"The trouble was usually of your own making," his mother reminded him. "You mustn't blame Miss Cartwright."

"I know. But golly, 'I will not bring snakes to school' three hundred times! Those three little snakes wouldn't hurt anybody. Scudder 'n Bill 'n I wouldn't have kept them if they were dangerous, for heaven's sake. And the Easter eggs made of soap — Miss Cartwright should have given us an A for hard work, carving all those eggs and putting chocolate on them. 'I will never again make Easter eggs out of soap,' three hundred times. We almost wore out the blackboard writing sentences."

Clancy munched gloomily on a third piece of toast.

"And five hundred sentences for the chickenpox trick. That was the worst. How'd we know that Scudder really was going to break out with chickenpox the very next day? Boy, this has been a long year."

His mother sighed.

"It's been a long year for me, too, Clancy. I've never in my life made so many trips to the principal's office, and I don't intend to do it again," she added firmly. "You get through this one more day without

4

any funny business, you understand?"

"Oh, today'll be a breeze. No schoolwork at all, just promotion cards, and I know I'll get promoted."

Mrs. Chapman said, "Because Miss Cartwright couldn't take another year of it, I suppose."

"And we'll have the May Day exercises of course."

Mr. Chapman was amazed. "May Day? Ye gods, May Day on the tenth of June?"

Clancy explained patiently and a little sheepishly. "Well, it does seem sort of queer. Miss Johnson, the gym teacher, had us all drilled and trained and ready for May Day, and then she got chickenpox, remember? And it seemed a shame to waste all those weeks of practicing, so they decided to hold May Day on the last day of school, instead."

Mr. Chapman choked on his coffee. When he could speak again, he said, "I remember the chickenpox incident. You Tigers were held responsible, I believe."

"It's very hard to tell exactly where anybody gets a germ," Clancy defended himself. "The Tigers got blamed for it, but maybe they all picked it up from somewhere else — you can never tell, honest."

Clancy's best friends were Bill Brown and Scudder Williams. Together they made up the Terrible Tigers, the most exclusive and notorious club in the fifth grade. They were the guiding spirits behind much of the mischief in Mapleton's Elementary School, and were usually blamed for all of it.

The chickenpox incident had been Clancy's brain-

storm. On an unseasonably warm day in April, the Tigers had suddenly decided that they couldn't stand being cooped up in school one more minute. With pinkish paint from the art closet, they dotted their faces and arms during afternoon recess. When Miss Cartwright noticed the spots, she excused all three of them from class and hustled them home. It didn't take long for the three Tiger mothers to discover the hoax, and three well-disciplined Tigers went meekly back to school the next morning.

Miss Cartwright piled on the sentences, and the Tigers stayed inside at recess to write five hundred times, 'I will never again deceive my teacher and pretend to be sick in order to go home early.'

As they scratched away, Scudder remarked wearily, "I've written this so many times I really do feel sick. I feel awful."

As the day went on, Scudder felt worse and worse. His face was flushed, and his throbbing head felt heavy. Clancy urged him to tell the teacher, but Scudder whispered back that Miss Cartwright would never believe him.

So Scudder had tried to go on as usual. He sang in music class, shared his ice-cream cone at lunch with his twin, Lou-Ann. He had hard work keeping up with the class during the May Day practice, but he did the best he could. He forgot the steps and made so many mistakes that the girls were all snickering, and Miss Johnson had to lead him by the hand as they went through the last figures of the Maypole dance.

When Miss Cartwright had them all settled in their seats again after gym, she looked at his hot face and said firmly, "Scudder Williams! I should think you would have learned your lesson. Wash those paint spots off your face at once!"

"I can't wash them off," Scudder explained weakly. "I didn't put any on."

Scudder had chickenpox, the real thing this time. And he had spread it far and wide in Mapleton Elementary. Bill and Clancy got it, along with almost everyone else in the fifth grade. Miss Cartwright escaped, but Miss Johnson, who had somehow missed it as a child, got a hard case. It spread through every grade, and by the first of May there weren't enough well students to stage any kind of May Day celebration.

Perhaps it wasn't entirely fair to blame Scudder for the epidemic, but as Miss Cartwright pointed out to the principal, "If those Tigers hadn't pulled their smarty trick with the painted spots, I'd have noticed right away that Scudder wasn't feeling well. I could have sent him home before he seeded down the whole school."

It had been a hard year for the Tigers, and Clancy started off to school feeling relieved that it was almost over. He called back to his mother as he went down the front walk, "I forgot to tell you that all the parents are invited to this old May Day thing."

"Wait a minute," she answered. "Don't race off so fast. What time do we come?"

"Ten-thirty. Honest, it won't be very good. I just mentioned it because Miss Cartwright said we had to invite our parents."

"Well, you've invited me, and I've accepted," said his mother. "I've made the trip to school so many times this year because I was sent for, I'd like to do it once purely for pleasure. Tell Miss Cartwright I'll be there."

"Aw, gee," grumbled Clancy. Just then he heard a piercing whistle from the corner, so he waved hastily, hitched up his low-slung knee pants, hauled on a stocking that had started to slip, checked to make sure his mouth organ was in his hip pocket, and ran to meet Scudder and Bill.

As Clancy hurried up, Scudder put the last of a doughnut in his mouth and handed another to Clancy.

"Always eating," marveled Clancy. "I don't see how you can do it."

Scudder mumbled through his doughnut, "I have to eat to keep up my strength. I burn up a lot of energy just trying to keep alive with that bunch of girls around. Even the cat is a girl, and she has nothing but girl kittens. My father and I eat out of desperation."

9

Scudder Williams was a short stocky boy with a blond crew cut, and at least a thousand freckles. There were six children in the Williams family, and Scudder was the only boy. Two of the girls were older, two were younger, and one was his twin, Lou-Ann. He felt that the whole situation was almost too much to bear.

"I'm surrounded by girls," he often moaned. "And

it's no use trying to ignore them. Girls are awful. They won't stay ignored."

Bill Brown was as different from Scudder as could be. He was dark-haired, and very tall for his age with long gangly legs that grew longer, so his mother said, by at least an inch a week. He peered nearsightedly out at the world from behind big round-framed glasses, yet he never missed a thing that was going on.

Bill was bright in school. He was always the first to finish a test, he always had perfect papers, and always knew the right answers in class. He could easily have been Miss Cartwright's pet if he hadn't been one of those Terrible Tigers.

He dreamed in class and made elaborate drawings of airplanes and trains while he was listening to the teacher with only one ear. His high-flying imagination was an asset to the Tigers Club, although more than once his high-flying chemistry experiments in the club's tree house had made the Tiger parents threaten to disband the group altogether.

The third Tiger was Clancy Chapman, and he came right in between the other two. Not as short and stocky as Scudder, not as tall and thin as Bill, with flaming red hair and the brownest brown eyes. He had a nice straightforward smile that made the angriest teacher forgive a lot. Even the hard-pressed Miss Cartwright had to admit that Clancy had many good qualities.

"He's very fair and honest," she said. "If he promises not to do something again, he never does. The

11

only thing is, he thinks up something brand-new to do, worse than before. And whatever he does, the other two do."

"Never mind, Miss Cartwright," the principal of Mapleton Elementary consoled her. "The Tigers will be in sixth grade next year, and Mr. Morrow will have to cope. You've only one more day to get through and then you can relax."

As it turned out, it was quite a day.

After the opening exercises on that last day of school, Miss Cartwright made a little speech about what a good year it had been and how sorry she would be to lose all her fine students, but never mind, they'd still be friends and must drop in and see her and let her know how they were making out in sixth grade, and now — the report cards!

Scudder and Clancy had done fairly well in their studies, mostly B's, except for a big black C in arithmetic for Scudder, and a B minus in spelling for Clancy. Bill's report was one A after another right down the list.

But all three groaned when they saw how Miss Cartwright rated them on Classroom Behavior, Cooperation, Attitude Toward Study, Willingness to Accept Correction, and Desire for Improvement.

"Gosh!" muttered Bill.

"Wow!" said Clancy. "She certainly didn't spare the horses."

12

Scudder gave a low whistle. Lou-Ann leaned over from the next seat.

"I got an A in geography," she said proudly. "What did you — oooooooh!" she almost shrieked, and then lowered her voice as Miss Cartwright looked her way.

"Ohhhhh, Scud! I've never seen such a horrible report. Wait till Dulcy sees —"

Scudder grabbed the yellow card and jammed it into his pocket. His face was very red. He sneaked a quick look at Clancy and Bill. Clancy looked sort of miserable, too, but Bill had recovered from the first shock and was as dreamy and unconcerned as ever.

"Now," Miss Cartwright was saying, "we'll all assemble on the playground for the May Day — I mean Closing Day — exercises. I know you'll all do beautifully and make me very proud of my fifth graders. Every one of my fifth graders, you understand," she added, with a grim look in the direction of the Tigers. "I'd just better be proud of every one of you."

Out on the playground, things began to look brighter. The sun was pleasantly warm, the sky was blue, and a nice brisk breeze was blowing. The parents were all sitting in the shade on folding chairs from the auditorium.

Clancy put all throughts of his report card out of his mind and concentrated on enjoying what was left of the last day of school.

There was a lot to enjoy. First there were relay races and then dumbbell drills and a scarf drill, and an exciting tumbling act by the fourth-grade boys. The fifth grade was lined up on one side to await their turn to perform.

"How'd we ever get into this Maypole dance business, anyway?" Scudder wanted to know. "Why couldn't our class do a good tumbling act or cartwheels or something?"

"Because we voted, remember? And there are fourteen girls in the class and only twelve boys," Clancy reminded him.

"That's democracy for you," laughed Miss Johnson. She was lining them all up with their partners. "The majority rules and the rest grin and bear it."

"That's girls for you." Scudder was disgusted. "If the girls are so anxious to hop around and show off I wish they'd do it and leave me out of it. I'm so mixed up I don't know if I go left first, or right."

A worried frown puckered Miss Johnson's forehead.

"Oh dear." Then she smiled again. "No problem at all, Scudder. Dodie Haines is taking a boy's part to make the partners come out even, and she knows every step perfectly. Clancy, you keep an eye on Dodie, and Scudder, you forget about left and right and do just as Clancy does, then Bill will follow, and nobody will have any trouble."

Dodie smirked over her shoulder at Clancy.

"Just watch me, Clancy. Just do whatever I do."

Dodie Haines was the Tigers Club's sworn enemy. The tree house where they held their secret meetings was strictly out of bounds for Dodie, and much as she longed to pry into the secret sounds and smells that came from the clubhouse, she knew better than to try.

But it irked her to be kept out of so much that seemed interesting, and so she got back at the Tigers every chance she could.

The music for the tumbling act had stopped and everyone clapped. Then Mr. Jones cranked the Victrola again, set the needle on the record, and Miss Johnson whispered encouragingly, "All right, now. Here you go."

They pranced out onto the playground in time to the music and took their positions around the Maypole. According to the plan, the bright colored streamers should have been hanging straight down within easy reach, but the breeze had changed the plans and the ribbons were flapping and blowing.

15

With only a little confusion, each boy and girl finally got hold of a streamer. At a nod from Miss Johnson, the dance began. Back and forth, over and

under, the streamers were woven together in a beautiful bright colored pattern that traveled down the pole as the ends of the streams grew shorter.

"Look at that Dodie," muttered Clancy. "Thinks she's a ballet dancer."

Dodie was indeed making the most of the occasion. The others had been told to watch her, so she was giving them something to watch. She pointed her toes, and she tripped gracefully around, smiling at her parents in the front row.

As she looked over her shoulder to make sure that Clancy was following her exactly, the breeze that was whipping the flag and the Mapleton school banner blew even harder. She was holding her ribbon delicately with her wrist gracefully arched, and a sudden gust of wind snatched it out of her hand.

Clancy had been plodding around in a far from graceful way, hoping that the dance would soon be over. Now he straightened up and started to grin as Dodie began to chase the elusive ribbon. He, too, let go of his ribbon, and the wind tossed it away above his head. Almost automatically, Scudder and Bill followed, and then the Tigers did exactly as Dodie did as she tried to catch her ribbon.

"You heard Miss Johnson," Clancy said as he ducked under Georgie Mears' arm. "She said to do whatever Dodie does."

Confused, Georgie hesitated, and his partner Emily

17

gave him an impatient shove. Philip bumped into him and tangled with Bill, who was leaping high to catch the end of his green ribbon. In a few seconds, the well-planned Maypole dance somehow turned into a shambles, with the boys all laughing and cavorting, and the girls huddled together in a furious group in the center.

The parents tried not to laugh, but when Bill Brown's old dog Patch suddenly joined the group, barking wildly and chasing the flying streamers, it was too much. Miss Cartwright hurried to turn off the music and motioned the fifth grade off the playground.

The joke that had seemed so funny out in the sunshine did not seem half so hilarious in the principal's office.

"Clancy, Scudder, Bill." He looked sternly at each one as he spoke. "I've dismissed the rest of the boys since it was very plain that they only followed your lead. But you three — you knew perfectly well what Miss Johnson meant when she said to do exactly as Dodie did."

The Tigers hung their heads. They knew that Mr. Jones was right.

"We-ell," he said thoughtfully, "since this is the last day of school, I can't very well keep you in, or assign any homework, but we can't let this incident pass, either. Miss Cartwright has had her hands full all year long with you boys, one thing right after another.

Your report cards," he glanced at the cards on the desk in front of him, "certainly prove that. There's a lot to be desired as far as behavior is concerned.

"The way I see it," he went on, "you are pretty good fellows separately, but when you get together in this club of yours, things begin to happen. Maybe we'll have to outlaw the club and break up this combination. I don't intend to go through another year like this."

The Tigers looked at each other. No club? No meetings, no secret plans, no fun in the tree house?

"Gee whiz, Mr. Jones!" gasped Scudder. "The Tigers Club is the only thing that keeps me going! It's the only thing in the world that doesn't have girls in it!"

"Well, if it means that much to you, you'll have to do something to deserve it," said Mr. Jones firmly. "Let's leave it this way. If, by the end of the summer, you can prove to me that the Terrible Tigers can do something really worthwhile, carry out one plan that doesn't end up in trouble for somebody, then I'm all for the Tigers. Do it yourself with no help from anybody, you understand. But if you can't — that's the end of the club. I'm sure I can count on your parents to back me up and keep you apart after school hours if it seems necessary."

The sun was still shining brightly, the sky was as blue as ever, the same playful little breeze was blowing, but as far as the Tigers were concerned it was a dreadful day.

They walked home slowly in complete silence. For once, nobody had a thing to say. Mr. Jones had said it all.

2

REMEMBER, keep the yard in shape while we're gone, the grass, anyway. Horace'll help if the flower beds get ahead of you, or you can ask Scudder and Bill to pitch in. Sure you're not going to be lonesome, son?"

Clancy grinned. His father had gone over all these things at least three times in the past half hour. His mother had stopped her last-minute packing every time he came near, to hug him or smooth his red hair.

"Look, fellows, I'll be all right," he assured them. "I'm not a baby. I'm ten years old. And I'll have plenty of supervision. Grandma'll keep me in line."

"Grandma's not going to have to keep you in line," said his father firmly. "She's close to ninety, and while she's a real live wire, you're supposed to look out for her, not the other way around. You are not to make one bit of extra work or worry for her. Promise me, Clancy, and while you are promising, I want your solemn word that you won't let Grandma get involved with the Fourth of July celebration. You know how she gets carried away. Do you remember the year she decorated your bike and rode in the parade? She's not young, don't forget that, and we don't want her to overdo. So you do your best, Clancy, and promise me you'll take good care of her."

Clancy's mother looked troubled. She said, "George, I just can't go. You go on alone, and I'll stay here and keep an eye on Clancy and Grandma. I won't draw an easy breath the whole time we're gone."

"Please, Mother, you go on and have a good time. I'll be good, honest, and I'll take care of Grandma, too. Look, I'll give my solemn Tigers Club oath that I'll behave, and I'll do everything that you told me, and two months from now when you come home, everything will be in apple-pie order. Tiger's honor."

So Clancy's mother finished her packing, and they tended to all the odds and ends that were left undone. His father checked all the doors, left the note for the milkman, and closed the carriage-house-turned-garage.

Clancy tried to keep his tone offhanded as he said, "We'll be glad to keep the car dusted and polished. We can keep an eye on the tires and check the battery, too, just to see if she turns over —"

"Nothing doing," his father said firmly. "No playing in the car at all. No blowing the horn, no touching the car, even. One thing leads to another, and the first thing you know, the Tigers would find a good reason for trying to drive it down Main Street."

His father looked at the door.

"Actually," he said, "I can't think of anything you'll need out of here, so you won't have to come in and be tempted. The lawn mower will be in the shed, out of the rain, and so will the garden tools. Remember the rule — stay out of the tree house while we're gone. Someone might fall. Promise?"

Clancy sniffed scornfully.

"OK, if you say so, but no one ever did fall except Dodie, that time she sneaked up there. She's so dumb she falls off curbs."

Clancy's clothes and books, his turtles, his rock collection, and all of his other treasures, except, of course, for his mouth organ, were already in his tiny attic room down at Grandma Chapman's. His mouth organ was with him constantly. He had even been known to sleep with it in his pajama pocket. Jelly had officially moved down the day before, but he was an extremely independent cat and would no doubt come back up the hill to his usual hunting grounds.

When his parents were ready, when they could think of no more last-minute instructions and warnings, when Horace had come in his jiggly Model T Ford to take all the baggage to the station, the Chapman family walked down the hill to Grandma's little gingerbread house on Main Street.

Clancy and his mother and father lived in a good-sized house up on Crocker Hill Road, but Great-

grandma Chapman lived three blocks away, down on Main Street. Hers was the tiniest house in town, just the right size for one little old lady living all by herself. It had been built about fifty years ago in 1870, when fancy cut-out wooden trim was the latest thing on the most up-to-date houses. Grandma's house fairly dripped with gingerbread from the eaves, and the windows and the porch roof. It was so fancy that people in town called it the gingerbread house.

It was like her, somehow, funny and fussy with unexpected gables and a miniature cupola on top. And like her too, in that it was solid and well built and strong, for all its eccentricities.

Downstairs there was a big kitchen that did for a living room and dining room, too, and a little front room that Grandma called her settin' room. It was a treasure house of interesting old-fashioned things, among them a stereopticon viewer, the collection of birds' eggs that Clancy's grandfather had gathered when he was a boy, fat albums of yellowed photographs, and a wheezy parlor organ.

Upstairs was Grandma's room and a big closet that had been turned into a bathroom, and Clancy's room. His room was almost like an afterthought, tucked under one of the gables of the roof. His bed was narrow — there was room for only a cot. But it was comfortable and covered with an old crazy-quilt that Grandma said didn't have to be bothered about, and who cared if a boy put his feet on the bedspread?

25

Grandma had Horace Applegate put up shelves for Clancy's belongings and gave him a battered old sea chest to keep his clothes in. His Sunday suit hung behind the door and for the rest, he planned to wear as little as he could get away with.

The room was so small that the three Tigers could just about squeeze in, but far from being a defect, the boys felt that this added to its interest. The other two were almost envious of Clancy, who was to spend two whole months with Grandma.

Clancy walked proudly down the hill beside his parents, his tall, redheaded father and pretty, dark-haired mother. He thought they looked rather special, for parents, and he thought he was rather special, too.

What other boy in Mapleton was being left in charge of a house and yard while his folks went to Europe? And what other boy had the oldest lady in town for his great-grandma? Especially such a nice old lady as Grandma was.

She was waiting for them on her front porch. She started to wave as she saw them coming down the tree-shaded street.

"Land's sakes," she greeted them. "I was beginning to think you were never coming. You'll miss your train for sure. Now let's get this goodbye business over with right now, and you two hustle on to the depot. Clancy and I'll stay here. I don't like saying goodbyes at the station unless I'm the one who's leaving on the train."

There was hugging and kissing all around, while Grandma fussed like a little banty hen.

"You'd think you were going to be gone two years instead of two months the way you're carrying on. Now Clancy and I'll get along just fine. No need to worry about us, is there, boy? Hurry now, the train won't wait and it's seven blocks to the station."

"Goodbye, goodbye! Don't forget to bring me a rock from every country you visit," shouted Clancy as his parents hurried down the street to the station.

27

When Mr. Chapman had suddenly learned that he would have to go to Europe on business, and when Mrs. Chapman had decided to go along, Grandma Chapman had said firmly, "Of course Clancy will stay with me. There's room for two in this little house, and we can be company for each other. Nobody's as good company as a ten-year-old boy. Any one of 'em has more horse sense than grown-up men four times their age. We'll have a good time."

Great-grandma Chapman was a tiny woman. She was dried and wrinkled, like an apple left in the attic over the winter. But little and old as she was, she was wiry and energetic and still full of enthusiasm for living. She was a "doing" kind of woman. If neighbors had sickness or bad news, she didn't just go to the front door with polite words of consolation, but knocked at the back door with an offer of help with the nursing, and a pie or a pot of her famous baked beans.

When she tied an apron around her middle and attacked a job, she put many a younger woman to shame. And she was without a doubt the funniest person Clancy knew. She had an inexhaustible supply of stories about things that had been happening in Mapleton for almost ninety years, things that only a person with a grand sense of humor would remember.

Clancy knew he was going to be happy at Grandma's, but still he had a strange empty feeling in his stomach as they sat on the front porch that evening. Grandma

28

rocked and hummed, while Clancy sat on the step and aimlessly kicked at a clump of grass.

He tried to guess where his mother and father were, and what they would be doing at that moment. They would be in New York, maybe, getting on the big ocean liner that was to take them to Europe. All of a sudden he felt a lot younger than ten, and awfully lonesome.

Just then his great-grandma said, "How about a pitcher of lemonade, first of the season?"

"No thanks, Grandma," he answered dully. "I'm not thirsty."

"Well, I'll make it anyway, in case you change your mind. Nothing like lemonade and sugar cookies to make you feel that summer is really underway."

She trotted briskly into the house, leaving Clancy sunk deep in misery on the step. The evening was warm and rich with the scent of all the roses and heavy-headed peonies in Mapleton. The streetlight on the corner shone through the leaves of the gnarled old oak tree, and cast wavery shadows on Grandma's white house. June bugs buzzed around the light, and moths fluttered in their dizzying summer dance. It was a lovely night, but when a familiar whistle sounded out of the dusk, Clancy was feeling too sorry for himself to answer.

"Hey, Clancy! Can you come out?" Scudder called from the gate.

"You don't have to yell," Clancy said, annoyed. "I'm sitting right here."

"Say, what's eating you?" Scudder came up the walk and dropped down on the step beside him. "You sound lower than a snake's belly."

Clancy didn't really know what was the matter.

Scudder went on, "I thought you said you wanted to stay here at your grandma's. I know I'd like it. Boy, what I'd do with two whole months away from that pack of girls in our house. Of course, Grandma is a sort of girl, too — but it's not the same."

Grandma came out on the porch as Scudder was talking. His eyes brightened as he saw what she was carrying.

"This place is a gold mine, Clancy," he said earnestly. "A whole plate of Grandma's sugar cookies and no competition. This is the way life was meant to be."

"What are you boys going to do this summer?" inquired Grandma. "Any big projects?"

"Mostly mess around," said Scudder, between mouthfuls of cookie. "We want to get in some fishing and swimming, and of course we've got to work out a plan to keep the Tigers Club from being broken up. We'll need something real special for that, won't we, Clancy?"

Clancy reached out in the dark to poke Scudder, but before he could say anything, another whistle sounded out by the gate.

"Come on in, Bill. We're just having some more refreshments," called Grandma. Then she said to Scudder, "Now, what were you saying about a plan to keep the Tigers from being broken up?"

Clancy tried again to signal Scudder to be quiet, but Scudder misunderstood and said, "Quit shovin', Clancy. I'll move over."

Clancy made room for Bill Brown on the step. With a Tiger seated on either side of him, he was beginning to feel more like himself again. He did hope that Bill's arrival would change the subject of conversation. With all the fuss about getting moved down to Grandma's, he hadn't had a chance to tell his friends about the important conclusions he had come to.

"Scudder means the plans for the Big Birthday Celebration, Grandma," Clancy said breathlessly. Scudder started to protest, "I wasn't talking about —" but Clancy hurried on.

"It's going to be a pip! They were going to have

31

just the regular Fourth of July parade, but then someone figured out that Mapleton is two hundred years
old this summer, 1722 to 1922, so they're going to com-
bine the Fourth of July and the birthday and make it
into one big celebration."

"Boy, what a wing-ding that'll be!" said Bill. "A
parade, and fireworks, and a big supper at the Fire
House, and speeches and a prize, too."

Grandma wanted to know what the prize was for,
and Bill explained, "For the most unusual and original
way of celebrating the town's birthday, like fixing up
your house — you know, bunting and flags, or fancy
colonial costumes on everybody, or — well, whatever
anybody can think of for a 200th anniversary."

"I'll bet we could think of something." Grandma
was rocking faster, and even in the dark, Clancy knew
that her eyes must be sparkling and he realized that
he had made a bad mistake. He stood up abruptly.

"I've been sitting around all evening. I need some
exercise. How about a race?"

Bill protested that he had just gotten there and had
had only one cookie, but Scudder remarked that the
step was getting pretty hard.

"Where do you want to race to?"

"Town square and back."

So off they went, out the gate and down the street.
As soon as they were out of sight of Grandma's porch,
Clancy stopped.

"I thought you wanted exercise," puffed Scudder.

"What I really want is a Tiger meeting. I've been thinking."

"A very good hobby," said Bill judiciously. "More people ought to take it up."

"We have to think of a plan to square the Tigers Club with Mr. Jones, right?"

"Right."

"And whatever we think of, we have to carry out all by ourselves, right? Then whatever we think of, we can't tell Grandma about it, because she'd want to help right away, and Mr. Jones said no help. And I made a solemn promise that I wouldn't do one thing to make Grandma extra work. And we daren't let her get mixed up in this Birthday thing because that would be work, see? Don't see anything at all about the Fourth of July celebration and maybe she'll forget about it. But most of all, don't mention the Tigers' plan. Promise?"

When the other two had repeated the Tiger oath, Clancy drew a sigh of relief. A big load had dropped from his shoulders.

"We can make some good plans tomorrow," he said. "Let's pack a lunch and go to Horsetail Creek and get our strategy all worked out while we fish."

The whole long happy summer stretched out before them as they strolled back to Grandma's. Plenty of fishing, plenty of swimming, plenty of just messin' around.

Bill and Scudder called goodnight to Grandma and

went on home. Clancy felt good again, so good that he ate all the rest of the cookies on the plate and drained the pitcher of lemonade. The old lady grinned at her great-grandson.

"Anybody who can eat like that isn't in danger of pining away from homesickness," she said. "Now scoot up to bed," she added sternly, "and no lallygagging. It's bedtime."

Clancy scooted. You didn't argue with Grandma. Upstairs in his cozy little room he stretched out in bed and looked up at the ceiling. In the winter the room was warmed by the heat that rose from the "settin' room" stove through a fancy iron register in the floor. The stove was cold now, but Grandma had thoughtfully set a lamp on the table below the register. The light shone through the iron grille in a lacy pattern on his bedroom ceiling, like ferns and leaves.

Clancy was too old to need a night-light, but the shadows gave him something to think about as he fell asleep. There was no time to remember that his mother and father were far away and getting farther every minute. He thought of ferns and leaves and woodsy things that reminded him of picnics, and picnics reminded him of — he reached out for the mouth organ that he had tucked under his pillow and played a few sleepy bars of a tune that sounded like picnics. Not more than a few bars, though, for in a minute he was fast asleep.

34

Downstairs Grandma listened and as the music faded off into silence, she smiled and turned out the "settin' room" lamp. Clancy was going to be all right.

3

Clancy awoke the next morning to the sound of rattles and bangs from the kitchen. He jumped out of bed and hurried into an old shirt and a new pair of overalls from his sea chest. Then he thumped down the steep winding steps into the kitchen.

"Morning, Grandma," he said. "Here, I'm supposed to do that."

He took the coal shovel from her hand and began to scoop out the ashes from the big coal stove.

"Go easy," Grandma warned, "or you'll have ashes all over the place. I was going to let you sleep for a while to celebrate the first day of your visit."

Clancy shook his head. "Too bad to waste a minute of vacation just sleeping. Us Tigers have plans."

He finished cleaning out the ashpit and carried the ashes outside to the big can in the shed. Jelly had laid his morning contribution of two dead field mice on the back doorstep so Clancy knew that the visiting cat felt at home. Clancy scooped them up expertly out of long practice and put them in the trash. This was one of Jelly's less endearing habits, but one that nothing could change. He enjoyed hunting and brought his prize home each morning for his family to admire.

Clancy carried in a pail of coal and an armload of kindling wood. Grandma had already poked up the fire and had a good hot bed of coals glowing beneath the stove lids, but she would have kindling and coal ready when she needed it the next time. The teakettle was bubbling away, the fire cracked and snapped, the iron griddle was heating and Grandma was mixing pancake batter.

In Clancy's house up on Crocker Hill, they had a gas range. Clancy's mother had tried to convince Grandma that it would be an improvement over her old coal stove. But Grandma was not impressed.

"I know this stove and it knows me, and together we turn out some mighty light biscuits. Besides, Peanut Butter would miss it. I couldn't upset his way of life. Cats don't care for change and neither do I."

The two big cats, Peanut Butter and Jelly, were eating their breakfasts out of blue and white saucers

37

on the floor. Soon Peanut Butter, Grandma's old yellow cat, would retire to the warm space behind the oven to clean himself. Jelly was younger but even bigger, black and shiny. He would squeeze behind the geranium pots and lie on the windowsill on his back with all four paws up in the air. It was a most un-cat-like pose, but Jelly always did things his own way, just as Grandma did.

Grandma had no objection to some changes. She had been one of the first people in Mapleton to have town water installed, and she said she never for a minute missed her old hand pump. But the coal stove stayed, old-fashioned or not. Clancy or his father stopped in each day to carry in pails of coal, though Grandma said it wasn't necessary.

"I'm strong as a horse," she insisted. "You're treating me like an old woman."

Clancy was just sitting down to breakfast when Bill Brown and Patch came to the back door. Bill had had his breakfast, but at Grandma's urging he came in for a stack of pancakes, all buttery and sticky with syrup. Patch had to stay outside, for Jelly bullied him unmercifully. When both boys were so full they couldn't eat another bite, Grandma said, "Well now, what are you up to today?"

"If you don't need me around here for anything, we'd like to go up to Horsetail Creek for some fishing," said Clancy.

"Go ahead," said Grandma. "The grass is mowed

and all the errands are run. Your father lugged home enough groceries to last through a long hard winter. Not a thing for you to do. You'll want a lunch packed, of course — unless maybe you're planning to cook your catch?" she added mischievously.

Bill grinned.

"We've been fishing in Horsetail Creek for years and never caught anything bigger than a minny. Mom fixed me a lunch just to be sure I don't starve."

As Grandma began to make his lunch Clancy asked her how Horsetail Creek got its funny name.

"It wasn't always called that, you know," she answered. "Only for the last eighty years or so. Before that it was Winding Creek — still is, farther up in the county. Folks call it Horsetail because of a city fellow, a traveling salesman or some such, who stopped to let his horse take a drink. It was spring, and the muddy bank gave way, and the horse went into the creek. He wasn't in any danger — the creek wasn't deep and the horse was just standing there up to his knees. But the city fellow got excited and started hollering and yelling until they could hear him clear to Judson's farmhouse — that would be Mr. Judson's grandfather, you know, — "

Grandma stopped making sandwiches to laugh.

"He grabbed that big horse by the tail and pulled until he hauled the poor critter backwards right out of the water and up on the bank. It's been called Horsetail Creek ever since."

"Gosh, Grandma, this is enough lunch for an army," said Clancy as Grandma packed apples and cookies and sandwiches in a big bag. "But we'll be able to eat it all," he added hastily.

"Now out of my way, both of you." Grandma bustled around the kitchen. "You may not have chores, but I do. It's ironing day, and besides that, this cookie jar is almost empty. Out!" She opened the screen door and pointed. They went out.

Scudder still hadn't shown up, but it didn't matter, since they weren't in any real hurry anyway. Patch rolled over in the sunshine and let Bill scratch his ears. Clancy rubbed dirt into his brand-new sneakers. He slid back and forth on the step to soften his overalls.

"If there's anything I hate, its new overalls," he explained to Bill. "Mom got me outfitted with these new stiff ones and threw away all my old ones that felt good. She said she didn't want Grandma to spend all summer keeping the seat of my pants mended."

"That's always the way," said Bill. "Just when pants begin to feel good, mothers get ashamed of the way they look. I've got a pair all broken in perfectly, but I have to keep 'em hidden or my mother'll snatch 'em."

Just then Scudder came panting into the yard with his fishing pole and tackle box.

"I thought I'd never get here," he puffed. "I was up early and all ready to go when Dulcy saw me and

Zowie! First thing I know I'm watching the baby. Girls!" he said disgustedly.

"Why couldn't Dulcy or Lou-Ann watch Susy?" asked Clancy.

"Because they're bossy old girls, I guess. They've got some big important plan going, getting ready for a picnic someplace. As if my plans weren't important too. Oh well, I finally got away. Let's go, before the wolf pack catches up with me."

Bill poked Patch gently with his foot. The old dog stretched and yawned, a loud yawn that was a peculiar sort of moan.

"He's the craziest yawner I ever saw," said Bill fondly. "No other dog in town yawns like that. Maybe no other dog in the world."

They gathered up the assorted pile of equipment they would need during the day, fishing poles, lunch boxes, a bone for Patch, Bill's field glasses —

"What do we need them for, on a fishing trip?" asked Scudder, as Bill slung them over his shoulder. "Flying fish?"

Bill didn't dignify this remark with an answer, but picked up his insect jar and butterfly net. Well loaded, they started out.

They hurried out the front gate and turned left up Main Street. A right turn would have taken them past houses set back from the street, past fences heavy with rambler roses, through the town Square and into the small business district of Mapleton. But they were headed in the other direction, up the hill and through the woods, and over the fields to Horsetail Creek. They made a detour through some back alleys to avoid Scudder's house, for fear the girls might see them, and breathed easier when they were past the last house in town. As they climbed Hunter Hill, Clancy said, "I wish I had a nickel for every time I've dragged a sled up this hill."

"We'd be millionaires," laughed Scudder. "Sure is a nice hill for coasting."

"I got going once last winter and slid all the way down Main Street to the Square. That's just about the record," said Bill proudly.

"Just about," agreed Clancy. "Joey Haines went as far as Hadley's drugstore, but he had a bobsled."

"And he's fourteen," said Scudder. "I'll bet when we're fourteen we'll be able to go past the Fire House. Say, did you ever notice how a good family gets all messed up when they have girls? Take Joey — he's a good guy. He must feel terrible being a brother to a stupe like Dodie Haines. She's even worse than my sisters and that's pretty bad."

They all sympathized with Scudder, but there was nothing anyone could do. Girls were girls and that's all there was to it.

The woods at the top of Hunter Hill smelled cool and damp, like mushrooms and wet leaves. Squirrels chattered at them from the treetops, and a blue jay scolded as he went by. There was a path, but they didn't bother to follow it. They knew every inch of the woods by heart. They took a short cut that brought them out into a clearing and then down along the edge of Farmer Judson's plowed fields and across the meadow to the creek.

Horsetail Creek wasn't a big creek, not very deep at its deepest. Mostly it rippled and sang over the rocks and gathered occasionally in little pools where a fish might be hiding or might not be.

It was fun to be fishing again, even if the fish weren't biting. They didn't have a nibble. Not even a little silver minnow came up to investigate the bait. But the Tigers didn't care. The sun was warm and bright, the water splashed cool on their bare feet.

Old Patch wandered away to sniff out a rabbit's trail but soon came back to sleep in the sun on the creek bank. It was a good day. Finally Clancy said, "Isn't anyone else hungry? I'm starved."

Bill squinted up at the sun. "So'm I, but I don't think it's noon yet. The sun isn't overhead."

Scudder rubbed his stomach. "Always the scientist. Who cares where the sun is? Let's eat."

So they spread out their lunch on the grass. When Clancy opened his bag, Scudder said "Wow!"

"Yep, my grandma doesn't do things halfway. She sure packs a lunch."

They traded back and forth, Scudder's pickle for Bill's carrot strips, a tunafish sandwich for a cheese and ham. Clancy had more than enough cookies to go around several times. At last they stretched out on the bank, stuffed.

Scudder lay on his back with his hands behind his head, lazily looking up at the fat white clouds in the blue sky. Clancy started to play "Marching through

44

Georgia" on his mouth organ and then gave it up as too energetic.

The creek bank was cushioned with soft new grass and sprinkled with daisies and dandelions. A few white cabbage butterflies drifted over their heads, and a preoccupied beetle scurried by and never even noticed they were there.

Bill was on his stomach examining a patch of grass with the magnifying glass he always carried with him. He crumbled the remains of the last cookie into the grass and then gave the other two a running account of the activities of the ants that gathered.

Soon, though, with the warm sun and the big lunch, even Bill's scientific interest faded. His report came slower and slower and finally stopped altogether. After a few minutes Clancy said drowsily, "I'll go to sleep if I stay here. Let's go look for rocks for the collection."

"Aw," protested Scudder, "I can't move. You two go if you want."

So Bill and Clancy started out, wading down the creek and keeping a sharp eye out for especially nice stones. Clancy found a good one, dark green with white stripes, but when he dried it off to show it to Bill, he was disappointed to find that it had lost most of its pretty color.

Clancy was a rock collector, but he prized his finds because of their unusual shape or color, or as a souvenir of the place they had been found. Bill's interest was more scholarly. He could identify all the varieties of stone that were found in the region of Mapleton, and he knew how they had been formed millions of years ago. But today he was full and lazy, and just looked for stones that were different from any that Clancy had already collected.

There was a shout and a bark behind them. Scudder and Patch had decided to wake up and join them.

"Wait up for me," shouted Scudder. "These rocks are sharp on my feet. Oh! Ouch! Galloping goldfishes!"

"What's the matter?" asked Clancy. "Did you stub your toe?"

"Stub it! I broke it right off, I think. This blooming red stone here — "

Clancy looked closely at the stone.

"It's a beauty! Boy, this is swell!"

"Swell? I break my toe, maybe my whole leg, and you say it's swell!" complained Scudder.

"The stone, not the toe. You'll live, Scud. You always do. Say, what's that? Listen — "

There was the sound of voices coming. They all stood still and listened. Then they saw a group of girls with picnic baskets coming across the field.

"OH no," groaned Scudder. "Dodie Haines and that Allen girl and my sisters, all five of them! Let's get out of here before they see us."

Clancy thought quickly.

"Bend down low under the creek bank, and we'll

sneak over to that old sheep shed of Judson's. We can make it if we hurry."

They went as fast as they could on all fours. Even Scudder hurried, his stubbed toe forgotten. Low brush hid them from view until they were almost to the tumbledown shed at the edge of the pasture. They made a dash for the shed across the open space, and disappeared around the corner and into it.

"That was close," panted Clancy.

"Sure was," agreed Scudder. "If the wolf pack had seen us we'd have ended up taking care of Susy. Good-bye fun."

They could see the girls plainly through the cracks in the wall. There were the five Williams girls, Scudder's sisters. Dulcy, who was thirteen and a pretty curly-haired girl, was the oldest. Next came Pat, curly-haired also, but fair, instead of dark-haired. Then Lou-Ann, ten, with long straight hair, as blond as Scudder's crew cut. Then Mary, with braids, a lively seven. And little Susy, the four-year-old baby of the family.

The other girls were Dodie Haines and Emily Allen. Dodie, they felt, made their lives a "real fat mess," but plump little Emily Allen wasn't too bad. At least she didn't go out of her way to be obnoxious, but she was a girl, and that was enough for the Tigers.

"How're we going to get out of here?" asked Bill after they had watched the girls for a while. "We don't want to stay cooped up in here all afternoon.

We should have run in the other direction!"

"Maybe they'll leave," said Clancy hopefully. But they soon saw that the girls had settled down to stay. They spread out a tablecloth and opened all the baskets.

"Look," Scudder muttered indignantly. "They've got a whole chocolate cake. And it looks as if they brought a pie, too!"

The girls ate a leisurely lunch. It seemed to the hidden Tigers as if they went on eating forever. Bill kept asking when they would finish, and if girls always ate this slowly. Bill had a younger brother. He had no experience at all with sisters.

"Girls always do just the opposite of what you want 'em to do," said Scudder disgustedly. "They're poison."

"Ssh," said Clancy. "They'll hear us. Are they going away?"

"Naw, just taking off their shoes to go wading."

Patch, who had settled down on a pile of hay in the sheep shed for another of his naps, woke up just then. He stretched and yawned his moaning yawn. It sounded louder than usual inside the shed.

Dulcy stopped untying her sneakers and looked quickly over her shoulder at the building.

"Sssshhh!" Bill tried to keep the old dog quiet. "They'll be on us like a swarm of bees if they find out we're here."

"I think that's how we'll get rid of them," whispered

Clancy. "Can you make Patch do that again?"

"No, he never does it unless he's just waking up."

"Then we will. Start moaning quietly and gradually get louder."

"Ghosts." Scudder was delighted. "All girls are scared to death of ghosts. They'll think this old place is haunted."

The Tigers began to moan softly. Dulcy looked again at the shed and said something to the others. The moaning grew louder and died down again. The girls crowded closer together and looked worried.

"Let's not overdo this," whispered Clancy. "Go easy so they don't catch on."

They waited a few minutes and began to moan again.

The girls started to gather up the remains of their lunch. Scudder began to giggle.

"Stop it!" whispered Bill. "You'll give the whole scheme away!" But once he was started, Scudder couldn't stop giggling. His moans quivered and quavered and grew louder. Bill tried to put his hand over Scudder's mouth to muffle the giggles. So did Clancy. Somehow in the scuffle, one of them stepped on Scudder's sore toe.

"OWEEEEEEEEEEEEEEE — !!"

At the sound of Scudder's bloodcurdling scream, the group of girls dropped everything and ran. They scooted pell-mell through the pasture, over the stone wall, and into the woods. The big ones dragged the little ones, and in a flash, all of them were out of sight.

All three of the Tigers laughed then. They howled and squawked and rolled on the floor. They had never laughed so hard. Finally Clancy sat up and wiped his eyes.

"We've gotta get out of here. If they get brave and come back for their baskets and find us — oh boy!"

"Let's take their baskets and shoes along. Then if they come back, they'll really believe that ghosts came and spirited their things away."

As quickly as they could, the boys gathered up the picnic things and the assorted pairs of shoes and sneakers. Well loaded down, they hurried back along the creek bank, up around the bend where they had left their fishing poles and tackle boxes. Then they skulked back into the woods, keeping out of sight as much as possible.

They took the long way home through the woods

so as not to meet the girls. When they reached Scudder's house they stopped behind the garage while Scudder went ahead to make sure the coast was clear.

He was back in a minute, grinning from ear to ear.

"They're all in the kitchen, telling Mom about the ghosts in the haunted barn. Excited as a bunch of old hens. Seems that after a while Dulcy and Lou-Ann and Pat got up nerve enough to go back for the shoes, and when they found everything was gone they were more scared than ever."

The Tigers tiptoed up to the back porch and lined up the shoes and baskets neatly on the steps. Scudder's giggles started to break loose again but the chatter in the kitchen was loud enough to cover any noise outside.

Then they hustled around to the front. Scudder called goodbye and went in the front door as cool and innocent as you please.

Grandma was rocking on the porch as Clancy came in the gate.

"Have a good day?" she asked.

"Swell!" said Clancy happily. "A real Tiger of a day!"

4

SEVERAL busy days went by, and Grandma said nothing
at all about the Fourth of July celebration. Clancy
decided that she had forgotten about it, or else had
lost interest. It didn't seem like Grandma to lose interest, but at any rate she hadn't mentioned it. Clancy
was relieved.

"After all," he said to Bill and Scudder, "I can't out-
and-out forbid her to do anything. All I really can
do is discourage her, and she doesn't discourage easy,
let me tell you."

All went well until one afternoon when Clancy and
Grandma were on their hands and knees weeding the
flower bed that bordered the front walk. A day of
warm rain had sent the young plants shooting up, and
the weeds, too. It was hard work, but Clancy rather
enjoyed weeding with Grandma. She knew wonderful
stories about the old days, stories of the things that
she did when she was Clancy's age.

Clancy straightened up to rest his back, then said in a low voice, "Don't look now, Grandma, but Mrs. Holloway is coming down the street all dressed up. Looks as if she's coming to visit us. She has on her visiting hat, the one with the cherries on it."

"Keep your head down," hissed Grandma. "Maybe she won't notice us. Maybe she'll go on by."

But Mrs. Holloway did notice them and turned in at the gate. Grandma grunted and got to her feet. Clancy whispered, "I'm getting out of here as fast as I can."

"I would if I could," Grandma answered. "That woman — " She picked up the worn cushion she had been kneeling on and gave it a vigorous shake, as if she would like to do the same to Mrs. Holloway.

Mrs. Holloway was saying in a syrupy voice, "Well, well, Mrs. Chapman, aren't you the naughty one to be doing such hard work in this hot sun?" She shook her finger at Grandma, and added as if she were talking to a baby, "We must take care of ourselves, you know. We aren't as young as we once were." Then she turned to Clancy.

"And here's Clarence. What a fine little chap you've grown to be, sonny."

Clancy's face flushed as red as his hair. If there were two words in this world that he really hated, one was Clarence and the other was sonny. Why his folks had named him Clarence he'd never understand. Luckily Grandma had come to his rescue when he was only a

baby and had started to call him Clancy. By now people had forgotten he had any other name. Except for an occasional Sunday school teacher, and Mrs. Holloway, who never forgot anything.

Grandma knew how annoyed he was. She said gently, "Maybe Mrs. Holloway would like some iced tea, Clancy."

He was grateful for a chance to get away before he said anything rude. Out in the kitchen he took his time about getting the iced tea.

Let her wait, he thought grumpily. Let her get real good and thirsty. He watered the geraniums on the windowsill. He wiped up some sugar that had spilled on the table. He fed his turtles and stood for a long time in front of the aquarium. Thoughtfully, he took little Timothy Turtle out of the water and dropped him in his shirt pocket, although he couldn't have said just what for. After a while he went back out to the porch with the pitcher and glasses.

Mrs. Holloway was a large commanding woman who was used to speaking her mind plainly, although often in playful babytalk, and to having her own way. She had a small obedient husband and a small obedient hired girl, and neither one of them had ever been known to talk back. Perhaps they would have, Clancy thought, if they could have gotten a word in edgewise. The Holloways were rather well-to-do, and this, in Mrs. Holloway's opinion, made her the social and cultural leader of Mapleton. She favored enormous

hats and a multitude of pins and necklaces and brace-
lets, and when she was dressed up to pay an afternoon
call she was an awesome sight.

She was saying, "Of course, I suppose they did want
to go, but it hardly seems fair to have those two young
people vacationing all over Europe while you are saddled with the care of their child."

Grandma was angry now, too. Clancy could tell by
the very straight way she held her back and the clipped
way she spoke.

"I don't feel saddled, Mrs. Holloway. I'm delighted
to have my great-grandson spend the summer with
me."

Mrs. Holloway laughed a trilling little laugh.

"Oh, you dear old proud thing, you. You wouldn't
admit to a soul that you've been imposed upon. But
you can't put anything over on Alice Holloway. No
indeedy! And here's Clarence with the tea. My,
doesn't it look delicious!"

Neither Grandma nor Clancy had much to say, but
that didn't bother Mrs. Holloway. There would have
been no opportunity to say it anyway. Clancy had
been planning to excuse himself and go over to Scudder's house, but there never seemed to be a break in
the steady flow of talk. She rattled along about one
subject and another. Clancy hardly listened.

Then he straightened up with a start as Mrs. Holloway said, "Are you and this dear little great-grandson
planning to enter the Birthday Competition? Oh my

dearie, I hope so. We want everybody in town to do *something*, just some flags or bunting or some little simple thing to show how proud we are of our town. Of course, the Holloway family has a great big exciting secret plan that I'm not going to breathe to a soul, and it may be that we'll win the prize, but don't let that discourage you. You could have a lot of fun trying, you know. And it's the trying that's fun, I always say. Be a good sport, win or lose, is my motto."

Clancy choked on his iced tea. This was all Grandma needed. After a speech like that she would walk a tightrope across Niagara Falls just to show Mrs. Holloway she could. He had to do something quickly to change the subject!

"More tea, Mrs. Holloway?"

"Thank you, Clarence, dear, I will. It's so very goody-good-good!"

Something slid out of Clancy's shirt pocket as he bent over to pour the tea, but Mrs. Holloway was so busy talking that she didn't notice the small splash in her glass.

Afterwards, Clancy explained it to Scudder and Bill.

"I really didn't do it deliberately, but when she started to drink the tea, and Timothy Turtle clinked against her teeth, and she began to yell bloody murder — there never was a chance to explain that it was an accident. She was hollerin' like a banshee. Nobody could say anything."

Scudder said in an awed voice, "They heard her clear down to the hardware store. The Volunteers thought it was an alarm and started to run the engine out of the Fire House. Nobody ever *heard* such screaming."

"I wish we'd been there," sighed Bill enviously. "What did your grandma say?"

"That's the funny thing. She didn't say a word for a long time after Mrs. Holloway stormed out the gate. Just sat in her chair and rocked and smiled. Then she got up and said she thought there was still time to make me a chocolate cake and I should get a quart of ice cream before supper. And she said to take good care of Timothy because she wanted him to live to a happy ripe old age."

"Gosh!" said Scudder. "What a day!"

"The trouble is, now Grandma's all stirred up about this Town Birthday Celebration. She wants to do something special to celebrate. What'll we do?"

Bill and Scudder didn't know the answer and neither did Clancy.

The next day was hot and muggy. Grandma said, "We're in for a storm. I can feel it in my bones."

"Which bones, Grandma? How does it feel?"

"Oh, it's just a feeling I've got. And the sunrise was red as fire this morning — that's a sure sign. You'd better hustle up to your house and cut the grass. If it rains for a day or so that grass will be so high you can't get through it with a mower."

Clancy didn't really want to cut the grass on such a sticky afternoon, but he knew that Grandma was right. And he had promised his father that he would keep everything shipshape.

"Maybe Scudder and Bill will come along, too."

Sure enough, when he whistled outside Scudder's house, Scudder came hurrying out to say that he'd be glad to help.

"If I don't, I'll have to cut the grass here," he explained, "and I sure hate to do that."

"What's the difference whether you cut it at my house or your house? The lawns are about the same size."

"I don't know, but there's a difference. Maybe it's because Dulcy and Pat always come out and complain that I'm poking. Anyway, I don't want to do it."

Bill and Patch were ambling along the street, and they were willing to come, too. Bill pulled out his shirttail and flapped it to make a breeze.

"Boy, this is a hot one," he complained. "Those clouds look like thunderheads. I bet we get rain before long."

Clancy got out the lawn mower and set to work.

60

Usually he mowed around and around the edges of the lawn in a neat square, being careful not to miss any strips of grass. But today he was feeling frisky. He began to do tricks with the lawn mower. He cut the grass in big figure eights, and then cut his initials. Then he wrote "Bill" in wobbly letters. Scudder wanted to try out some ideas so he cut a rabbit in the grass in the side lawn. Bill clamored for a turn, and he made a picture that he said was Patch chasing the rabbit, although it was hard to tell what it was. It was a good game and they were having a grand time until someone called, "Clancy Chapman, you're making a mess of that yard. I ought to tell your grandma!"

"It's old Dodie Haines," said Clancy, "but where is she?"

The Tigers looked all around, but they couldn't see Dodie anywhere.

"Ha, ha, you can't see me!"

"She's up in our tree house!" yelled Scudder. "You get down out of there!"

"You've got no business up there, Dodie Haines! That tree house belongs to us Tigers! Get out of there this minute!"

Dodie just laughed. "Make me," she taunted.

The enraged Tigers started for the ladder. Just in time Clancy remembered what his father had said — "Stay out of the tree house while we're gone."

"Wait a minute, fellows," said Clancy in a low voice. "We can't go up there. I promised we wouldn't."

61

"But how will we get that nutty Dodie to come down if we don't go up and make her?"

"I think I know. Hold it a minute."

Clancy ran around to the back shed. In a short time he was back again dragging the garden hose. Dodie was still taunting.

"Yah, yah, think you're so smart. You can't make me come down till I want to!"

Bill laughed. "Wait till she sees this! She'll soon want to."

Clancy pointed the hose up in the air, straight at Dodie.

"Now will you come down?"

"No!" Dodie yelled. As she leaned over the side of the platform and laughed, Clancy signaled. Bill turned on the faucet full force, and the stream of water hit her right in the face.

"Oh, oh!" she wailed. "You mean boys don't play fair! Stop it! You'll take all the curl out of my hair!"

"Will you come down?"

"Yes, you hateful things! I didn't want to play in your rickety old tree house, anyway!"

Dodie started down the first step of the ladder, but her wet hair hung down in her face. She couldn't see very well, and as she turned to look where she was going, her dress caught on a sharp limb.

"I'm stuck!" she howled. "I can't move, or I'll tear my new dress!"

"Too bad," said the unsympathetic Tigers, all together.

Dodie tried to twist free from the limb.

"See what you've done. You come up here and get me loose!" she commanded.

"We can't," Clancy explained cheerfully. "We'd like to help you, but I promised my father that we wouldn't go up in the tree house while they're away. You'll have to stay there until my folks come back from Europe."

"Ohhhhhhh — " she spluttered. "Boys are so horrible!"

There was a roll of distant thunder.

"We've got to get this lawn mowed before it rains. Let's get moving, Tigers."

They whizzed around the yard, taking turns with the mower until the grass was smooth and cut neatly. Clancy put the mower away and called, "So long Dodie, old neighbor, old friend!"

Bill asked in a low voice, "Are you really going to leave her there for two months, Clancy?"

"No, I guess not," Clancy answered.

"I would," said Scudder firmly.

"I don't suppose Dad would mind if I went up the ladder just to keep Dodie's new dress from tearing. In fact, I suppose he'd be pretty sore if I didn't. But let's give her a good scare first."

He called up to Dodie.

"I'm going to hurry home and write a letter to my dad and ask if it's all right for me to help you get down. I'll let you know as soon as I get an answer."

The Tigers started to walk away.

"He — lp, help!" called Dodie. "Please help me!"

"I'll send it special delivery to hurry it up," promised Clancy, while the other Tigers grinned. Thunder sounded again, closer this time.

"It's going to rain," she wailed, "and I'm scared of thunder and lightning."

"Oh, all right, but you don't deserve it."

Clancy climbed up and unhooked Dodie's dress from the limb. She hurried down the ladder, and raced across the lawn to the house next door. When she was safely out of reach, she called, "Just you wait, you Tigers! Some day you'll be sorry for the way you treat us girls!"

The Tigers laughed and laughed.

"Girls — phooey!" said Bill.

"Girls — poison!" said Clancy.

"Girls — are girls!" said Scudder. "We'll *never* be sorry!" Then they ran home through the first pelting raindrops, yelling at the top of their lungs,

"Dodie-o-podie, the bowlegged Dodie,

Tee-legged, tie-legged, toe-legged Dodie!"

5

FROM time to time the Tigers remembered their serious talk with Mr. Jones, and one of them would say idly, "We'd better think of a project to work on, a real worthwhile project. What'll it be?"

But no one had any ideas, and the pleasant summer days slipped by. Occasionally Clancy worried about it a little, but he didn't know what to do. He thought he had the answer to his worry when Grandma discovered a hole in one of the window screens.

"We'll have the whole mosquito population of Mapleton in here tonight if we don't get this mended. Clancy, will you ride over and see if Horace has time to fix it?"

Horace. Of course. Horace would have some ideas about a worthwhile project that would satisfy Mr. Jones.

Horace Applegate was the church custodian. He

66

kept the church cleaned up, and the lawn all neat and pretty with flowers. He was also Grandma's good friend and helper. He put up her screens and took down her storm windows and spaded her garden in the spring. Horace would know what to do.

Clancy found the tall gray-haired man over at the church, weeding the flower beds. First Clancy gave him the message about the screen so he'd be sure not to forget, and then he told him about the Tigers' problem.

Horace stopped his work and mopped his forehead with a big red bandanna handkerchief as he listened carefully.

"Seems to me you didn't exactly cover yourselves with glory this past year. I can see why Mr. Jones says you will have to redeem yourselves or break up the club altogether."

Clancy agreed unhappily.

"However," Horace went on, "having made a few mistakes, it doesn't mean you have to go right on making them. But whatever plan you think up, you must work it out all on your own, no one else can do it for you. And remember your promise to your father, don't let Grandma get involved in any extra work. That's important. Now you fellows think, and I'll think, and before long maybe we'll have a brainstorm."

Horace hadn't promised that he would think of an idea, just that he'd try, but Clancy felt better anyway.

67

He said goodbye to Horace and started to ride home down Green Lane, which was Bill Brown's street. Bill was out on the sidewalk oiling the scooter he had made out of an orange crate and some old roller skate wheels.

"Sure looks swell," said Clancy admiringly.

"She'll be even better when I give her a coat of red paint. The Red Devil, that's her name. Want to go down to the hardware store with me and get some paint?"

Clancy did, so they went around to Scudder's to pick him up, too.

Dulcy Williams was out in front of the Williams house, cutting some of the roses that grew all over their white picket fence, and talking with the McMichaels boy. Scudder hustled out to the walk when he saw the other Tigers coming up the street.

"Wanta see something horrible?" he greeted them. "Lookit old Googoo McMichaels making googoo eyes at Dulcy over the fence. I been watching them for twenty minutes and it's enough to turn your stummick."

"What're they doing?" asked Clancy with interest.

"First she says something about the weather and simpers, then he blushes and says, yes, it is a nice day and simpers. Then she pricks her finger on a rose thorn and he sympathizes as if she had cut her head off. She calls him Edward. Oh boy, it's awful!"

Clancy parked his bike and Bill left the Red Devil

68

at the curb, and they went closer to watch what Scudder assured them was a Disgusting Exhibition.

Dulcy and her caller gave an annoyed look at the audience and moved farther along the fence. The three edged up close again. Dulcy tossed her head

and said loudly, "A person can't even have a friendly conversation without those three little *funguses* hanging around!"

"Funguses!" muttered Scudder indignantly. "She calls *us* funguses and then talks to that creep — "

"Ouch," said Dulcy as she pricked herself on another rose thorn.

"Oooooo, Dulcy, have you hurt your 'ittle finger?" asked Clancy in a high false voice. "Let me look at it with my big googoo eyes and make it better."

The Tigers guffawed, but Dulcy and Googoo were not amused.

"Very funny," said Googoo coldly," for one so young and stupid. With all your wit and talent you ought to win the prize at the Birthday Celebration."

The Tigers laughed again.

"We must be leaving, Dulcy dear," said Bill. "We're going to the woods to cut you a be-yoo-tiful bouquet of skunk cabbage to wear to the opera."

This time Dulcy and Googoo looked really mad so the Tigers took themselves off down the street, still laughing.

"It's funny," said Bill. "There's Googoo, fourteen years old and acting like he'd lost most of his marbles. And then you take Joey Haines — he's fourteen, too, and he'd sooner die than talk to a girl."

"That's because he's got Dodie in his family," said Scudder wisely. "I wouldn't be surprised if Joey never said a word all his life to a girl — except maybe to a woman schoolteacher or something like that. That's how I'm going to be. How about you, Clance?"

Clancy wasn't listening. He was thinking about something that Googoo had said.

"Do you suppose we *could* win the prize in the celebration contest?"

"What's he talking about?" asked Bill.

"He's getting as loopy as Googoo," said Scudder.

"Listen," said Clancy impatiently. "I think maybe I have an idea. Couldn't we work out some good stunt and win the prize? Wouldn't that convince Mr. Jones that the Tigers Club isn't so bad?"

"Well — I guess — it'd have to be a pretty swell idea — but gee whiz, let's try. We've had some wonderful ideas in our day. Maybe we can come up with something this time." Bill was convinced.

"Suits me," agreed Scudder. "What'll we do?"

That was the question.

"Think about it hard," said Clancy. "We'll have a meeting tonight and make some plans. Whatever we do, we have to do it all ourselves, Mr. Jones said, and it has to be something that won't get us into trouble or the Tigers' goose is cooked."

They met that evening at the big tree that grew at the corner of Grandma's lawn, under the streetlight. The roots of the old tree were ideally suited for a meeting place. Each boy had his favorite niche between the twisted roots, and with their backs resting against the trunk they could have a private discussion

71

unnoticed in the shadows and yet see everything that went on up and down Main Street.

But at the meeting all their hard thinking got them nowhere.

"The ideas we have wouldn't win first prize at a dog show," said Clancy disgustedly. "We gotta have some sure-fire act that will knock everybody's eyes out."

"That's easy to say," said Scudder. "But we'll never win unless we get an idea that will beat Mrs. Holloway's. She's got a lulu, she bragged to my mother. Look, there's Mr. and Mrs. Farlow going to choir practice, most likely. They're going to be late. Mrs. Pettigrew went by ten minutes ago and she always makes it right on time."

Clancy was not to be distracted by the sight of the Farlows jogging down the street.

"Never mind Mrs. Pettigrew. What'll we do to win the prize at the Celebration?"

The Tigers went to bed that night with their question still unanswered.

"Mr. Farlow has some nice-looking watermelons in his store," said Clancy hopefully the next day.

"Good," Grandma answered. "My mouth's been watering for a melon. Could you bring one home, do you think? Mr. Farlow'll pick you out a good ripe one."

Clancy fastened his old red express wagon on behind his bike and rode down Main Street to Farlow's Fancy

Grocery. Mr. Farlow looked over the top of his glasses as Clancy clattered happily into the store.

"Well, well, Clancy Chapman. What do you hear from your folks, eh? They having a good time?"

"They sure are," said Clancy. "They're getting plenty of rocks for my collection. They've found a whole suitcaseful already."

"A suitcaseful? My, my. They *must* be having a good time with a whole suitcase full of rocks. And how is your great-grandma? She feeling sprightly?"

"She always is. She's the sprightliest old lady in Mapleton," said Clancy proudly.

"And the oldest, too. Say, I have a message for her. Will you tell her the Celebration Committee would be pleased if she would sit on the speakers' platform with the Mayor and the other bigwigs? We want her to be the guest of honor."

Then Mr. Farlow added anxiously, "She's not planning to be in the parade or anything, is she?"

"No sir!" said Clancy. "Not this year. She's just going to take it easy. I'll tell her about the speakers' platform. She'll be pleased, I'm sure."

"I'll stop by later and see her," said Mr. Farlow. "I do enjoy a visit with Mrs. Chapman. Now, what can I do for you, Clancy? Nice fresh vegetables, eggs, bread?"

"A watermelon, please. A big one."

Mr. Farlow thumped on several melons before he picked out a great big one. He cut a plug in it with his long knife and said that it was perfect, just right for eating that very day. Clancy and Mr. Farlow loaded it on the wagon. Clancy rode slowly and carefully so the melon would not roll out. He could hardly wait to get home with it.

"There's too much here for just the two of us," said Grandma when she saw the big watermelon. "Why don't you get the rest of the Tigers?"

Clancy didn't have to be asked twice. He was off like a shot to find Bill and Scudder. Scudder didn't have to be asked twice, either. He said sure he could come, soon as he finished licking the icing bowl. He generously offered Clancy the spoon to lick. Mrs. Williams was like Grandma — she always left a nice lot of frosting for licking purposes whenever she iced a cake.

Then the two of them hurried to Bill's house. Here they found things a bit more difficult. Mrs. Brown had left Buggy in Bill's care while she went to the store, and Buggy, in one of his lightning dashes for freedom, had somehow gotten away. He had headed straight for the house next door where the kitchen roof was being tarred. And being Buggy, he had naturally gotten into the thick of things. When Clancy and Scudder arrived, Bill was scrubbing furiously with sandsoap and a stiff brush while Buggy screamed that he was being skinned. It looked as if he might be, at that, for his fair skin was red as a beet in between the patches of tar.

"Let's take him home to Grandma," suggested Clancy. "I'll bet she knows how to get tar off. She knows just about everything."

So Bill left a note for his mother explaining that he and Buggy had gone to Grandma Chapman's for watermelon.

"We won't mention the tar just yet," he reasoned. "We'll cross that bridge when we come to it."

Grandma took one look at the tearstained, tar-stained little boy and knew exactly what had to be done.

"Lard," she said. "Nothing in the world cleans tar off like lard. Clancy, run down to the cellar and scoop some out of the lard pail — a whole cup of it. We'll need a lot to make a dent on Buggy here. And bring me one of those big old bath towels, too — and a handful of safety pins."

When he came back with all the equipment,

Grandma set to work. She peeled off Buggy's little blue sunsuit and made him a temporary covering out of the towel and the safety pins. Then she rubbed the lard generously into his hair and all over his tar-spotted face and hands and legs. It worked like magic, and in a few minutes Buggy was greasy but presentable again.

"There," said Grandma. "At least your poor mother won't fall down in a conniption when she sees you, Buggy. Now we'll clean your suit the same way and suds both of you off and we'll let the sun and the wind do the rest."

Grandma rubbed lard on Buggy's suit, then washed it out and hung it on the line to dry. Then they all settled down to their party.

It was a good watermelon party. There were as many thick juicy slices as anyone could eat, cut according to each one's size and appetite.

Buggy Brown, who was only four, and Grandma Chapman, who was almost ninety, had just medium-sized pieces. But Scudder and Bill and Clancy ate watermelon until it seemed to be dripping out of their ears. Patch didn't care for watermelon so he chewed happily on a bone that Grandma had saved for him.

They all lined up on the back steps and had a seed-spitting contest, which Scudder won easily.

"It's because I have this front tooth out." He grinned modestly.

Grandma wasn't a bit fussy about the juice and seeds

all over the back porch and walk. She said cheerfully, "Hose 'em off, Clancy. That's what water was made for, cleaning up the mess that watermelon makes."

Well, by the time they hosed off the porch and the steps and the walk, and then cleaned off their bare feet, everyone was pretty wet, anyway. So all of them except Grandma went under the hose for a good splash. Grandma swung in the hammock in the shade.

"Clancy," she said, "you deserve a Hip Hooray for thinking of watermelon. And Mr. Farlow deserves another for picking out such a good ripe sweet one."

Up to this minute Clancy had forgotten Mr. Farlow's message.

"Oh gee, Grandma, Mr. Farlow told me to tell you something — what was it now?"

He scratched his head and frowned as he tried to remember.

"Oh yes, the committee for the Celebration wants you to be the guest of honor because you're the oldest old lady in town. Isn't that nice?"

Grandma looked surprised. "Guest of honor?"

"Yep, you're to sit on the platform with the bigwigs. That's what Mr. Farlow said."

Clancy felt pleased as he told her. This was going to take care of one of his problems. Grandma would be a part of the Fourth of July Celebration without getting involved in any hard work. Grandma thought it was a nice idea, too.

"I guess I am the oldest resident, at that," she said, "although goodness knows I don't feel it. But it'll be fun to sit on the platform and get a good view of everything. And it won't interfere, either."

"Interfere with what?"

"Interfere with helping you fellows celebrate the Birthday. You're surely going to think up something in honor of the occasion, aren't you?"

"We — l-l," Clancy stammered as he looked quickly at the others. "I guess — so."

"I should hope so," she said briskly. "It'd certainly be a shame if we didn't all take notice that Mapleton is two hundred years old. It would look as if we didn't

78

even care. I'm looking forward to helping you work out whatever you want to do."

There was an embarrassing pause. Clancy knew it would hurt Grandma's feelings to tell her that her help was not needed, in fact was not even allowed. And he had no intention of telling her about the Tigers Club's disgrace at school, and of Mr. Jones's ultimatum. This was a secret he had told to no one but Horace.

So when Grandma made her offer of help, the Tigers didn't know what to say. Scudder and Bill looked at the ground and scuffed their feet awkwardly.

"We gotta go — I'll have to take Buggy home now — thanks for the watermelon —" Scudder and Bill mumbled. They took Buggy by the hand and hustled him, protesting, out of the yard. They didn't even wait to put on Buggy's suit, just dragged him along in his strange-looking towel costume. Patch gave a last regretful lick at his bone and followed.

Grandma looked startled at the sudden exit.

"That was a quick end to a party. What happened, anyway?"

Clancy didn't have an answer for this either. Grandma looked at him with those sharp old eyes that seemed to see right through him.

"What scared everyone off, I wonder?" she asked. "Is this younger generation getting soft? I've never known the Tigers to shy away from a little work —

and the celebration wouldn't really be work, only fun — "

Still Clancy had nothing to say.

Grandma looked at him again, then rumpled his red hair fondly and gave him a hug.

"Let's have an easy supper tonight, shall we?" was all she said. "I'm not very hungry — too full of watermelon."

6

G RANDMA CHAPMAN had been doing a lot of thinking about Clancy's odd behavior. She was pretty sure he was happy living there with her, and he certainly wasn't moping around missing his parents unduly. But what could his trouble be? His days seemed busy enough. He and his friends drifted from one pleasant occupation to another. Drifted — maybe that was it. Maybe they needed some organized activity. Grandma wasn't sure, but she kept the idea at the back of her mind and resolved to think of something.

"Looks as if your grandma has company," said Bill as the Tigers came in from a morning of "just messin' around." "There's some lady sitting on the porch with her."

"Maybe it's Mrs. Holloway," snickered Scudder.

"Fat chance," said Clancy. "She'll never show her face around here again. But let's go around to the backyard just in case it might be somebody just as bad. We can stay there until whoever it is leaves."

They opened the gate as quietly as possible and started around to the back but Grandma's visitor saw them.

"Oh, there you are, boys," she called. "I was hoping you'd come in from play before I left. You are just the ones I've been waiting to see."

Three Tiger hearts sank right down into their bare feet. Mrs. Daley was a nice kind woman, but she was the Sunday school Superintendent, and whatever she wanted them for, the boys felt sure they were not going to like it.

"Yes," she went on happily, "you three will do just fine. You're exactly the right height and everything."

Grandma explained, "The Ladies' Aid is putting on a pageant about the founding of Mapleton for the Birthday Celebration. Mrs. Daley is in charge."

"Pageant!" Clancy was alarmed. "Pageant! We don't want to be in any old pageant."

"Oh, nonsense," said Mrs. Daley, still happily. She sounded pretty sure of herself, as if the matter had already been settled. "You'll enjoy being in the pageant. We're all going to have scads of fun. And we need you, boys, we really do. After all, it's for Mapleton."

"I'm sure Clancy will be delighted to help you out," Grandma said briskly. "It is only proper to have the

Chapman family represented *somehow* in the Celebration."

Clancy wanted to say, "The Chapmans will be represented when the Tigers win the prize." But it was to be a surprise. He daren't even hint.

"Well, Clancy?" asked Grandma. "It's for Mapleton." She looked very firm. He knew he didn't have a chance if she had made up her mind. He nodded weakly and mumbled something.

"Bill? Scudder?"

The Tigers knew when they were licked. Bill and Scudder nodded too.

"If Clancy has to, we might as well," said Scudder gloomily.

"So it's all settled. First rehearsal is this afternoon at one-thirty. We're getting a terribly late start, but if we all work hard we can be ready in time." Mrs. Daley was very pleased. "You see," she admitted, "it's been a wee bit difficult to round up enough boys to take part. We have a lot of girls — they love dancing and dressing up and things like that — but not all boys take to it. We simply didn't have enough boys for partners in the dance, but everything is going to be fine, now."

Mrs. Daley said goodbye and went humming down the street, the daisies on her hat bobbing merrily. The Tigers were too horrified to move. At last Clancy sat down on the front step.

83

"Girls," he moaned. "Dancing and dressing up! Grandma, what kind of thing have you gotten us into?"

Even Grandma was dismayed.

"I — I thought Mrs. Daley said they needed pioneer boys to build the log cabin — nobody said anything about dancing — Where are you going, Scudder? Aren't you staying for lunch?"

Scudder shook his head firmly.

"No thanks, Grandma Chapman. I'm going home to pack my bag. I'm leavin' town."

He plodded away, walking like a discouraged old man.

"Wait," she called. "I'll think of something. I'll get you out of this somehow."

Scudder shook his head again, and waved a weary goodbye.

"We could catch something," suggested Bill. "Some serious disease — "

"The only thing that's going around right now is measles, and we've all had that."

"Then it's goodbye to our plan," said Bill. "We can't be prancing around in this old pageant and work out our idea, too — "

Clancy shushed him with a quick shake of his head and looked at Grandma. She hadn't heard. She looked as disturbed as the boys.

"I never dreamed," she said. "I guess my idea about organized activity was all wrong. We'll have to think of something."

Bill and Clancy and Grandma ate lunch in silence. No one was very hungry. Finally Grandma pushed back her chair.

"I'll get sick," she said. "I'll tell them I need you at home to look after me."

"That wouldn't do it," Clancy said practically. "If you said you were sick you'd have half the town in here bringing you jelly and hot soup, and they'd find out you were faking. Mrs. Holloway might even come to read poetry to you to lift up your thoughts. She did that to Mr. Hadley's wife once, and it made her sicker."

Grandma shuddered.

"Besides," said Bill, "that would only take care of Clancy. We've got to get me out of this, too. And Scudder, if he hasn't already left town."

"Well, we promised," Clancy groaned," so we'll have to go to one rehearsal anyway. But don't worry, we'll find a way out."

Clancy took his promises very seriously, and when he gave his word about something, he did it, no matter what.

It was a beautiful day. The sun was hot and bright and the big maple trees along Main Street cast a cool shade. There were a dozen things the boys could have been doing on a day like this, but instead they walked slowly and reluctantly down to the Town Square.

As Bill and Clancy cut through the little park in the center of the square, they found Scudder waiting for

85

them on a bench. He was knee-deep in gloom.

"We thought you'd left town."

"I couldn't," said Scudder. "I was planning to run away on the first freight through town, but when I got home my sisters were all talking about the pageant. It's even worse than we thought. I couldn't run out and leave you two to face it alone. After all, we're still Tigers. We have to stick together."

"What do we have to face?" asked Bill hollowly. "What — ?"

Scudder looked at them solemnly.

"This dancing," he said, "it's with partners, *girl partners,* and Dulcy says one of us will be just the right height for Dodie Haines."

"Not me," said Bill instantly. "I'll be too short. I'm going to cut off my head at the shoulders."

"It's no use," Scudder said. "That would make you just the right height for little old Emily Allen."

The basement of Town Hall was as busy as an anthill when the Tigers finally got up courage enough to walk in. The big room buzzed with excitement. Children were running everywhere while the women of the Ladies' Aid tried to keep order. Their flowered summer hats bobbed through the milling throng, and it was as if a strong wind was tossing a field of assorted violets and velvet roses and poppies.

Over at the piano Mrs. Hadley was struggling with the opening bars of "The Stars and Stripes Forever." She wasn't the town's best piano player, but she played the loudest, and was in great demand for public affairs.

"Ouch," Bill said as she played a crashing chord — a little bit off-key.

"If you can't hit it right, hit it hard! That's Mrs. Hadley's motto," muttered Clancy.

"This will be some affair with her playing and our dancing. The town'll never survive to celebrate another birthday."

The boys stood close together over in the corner of the big room, half hidden, they thought, by a rack of costumes. Bill was hopeful that perhaps nobody would notice them, that maybe Mrs. Daley would have forgotten all about them. She hadn't, though.

"Oh, boys, Clancy, Bill, Scudder — right over here, please, with the other pioneers," she called. They saw Philip Higgins and Georgie Mears and Smelly Schmell there, all looking miserable. And Googoo McMichaels standing close to Dulcy Williams, looking pleased.

As they crossed the room the Clark twins darted past them, with young Mrs. Bryant in hot pursuit. "Grab 'em," she panted, and the boys were glad to oblige. She was hot and mussed, with a big streak of chocolate down the front of her pink dress. She looked as if she, too, wished she were somewhere else.

"Thanks." She smiled when she had a wiggling twin held firmly in each hand. "If you boys haven't been given a part yet, come over and help me with the

87

little ones. I can use six extra hands right now."

But Mrs. Daley called again, "All pioneers over here, please." Mrs. Bryant sighed and dragged the reluctant twins back to the costume department to be fitted with Indian headdresses.

The pioneers that Mrs. Daley had managed to gather together were an assorted lot, all shapes and sizes. She was trying to stand the boys and girls together, back to back, to match them up for size.

Mr. Hadley had closed his drugstore long enough to run over and try on the fringed jacket that was to be his costume. He was going to be a pioneer father, Clancy gathered, who was building a cabin. The dancing was to take place at the house-raising. It was all very confused. Nobody seemed too sure what was going on.

Mrs. Farlow, the grocer's wife, was switching around in a long fancy dress, very pleased with herself, and Mrs. Daley was clasping her hands together and murmuring, "It's not the right costume at all for a pioneer woman — that's a ball gown. Oh dear, oh dear!"

Dulcy and Pat and Lou-Ann were to be pioneers, too. They frowned when they saw the Tigers. Dulcy told them very firmly that they were to behave themselves, no funny stuff.

"They needn't worry," whispered Scudder. "They don't know it, but we're not going to be here long enough to get into any trouble. We'll find a way out of this mess yet."

Clancy hoped so, but he was not at all sure how it could be managed.

"Quiet, everyone! Mrs. Fellows is going to say something," said Mrs. Daley. With the help of a few extra-loud piano chords from Mrs. Hadley, and shouts from the harassed members of the Pageant Committee, the big room finally came to order. Mrs. Fellows, a plump little lady with a high voice, scooted up on the platform and began to speak.

"I thought — the Committee thought — we all thought we'd be able to do a better job on the pageant if we knew what we were doing. Oh dear," she said nervously, "I don't mean that all you lovely people don't know what you are doing. I mean if we all had a clearer understanding of the history of our beautiful town — well, it stands to reason we could play our parts better if we knew what our parts were — " Thoroughly confused, she paused for breath and then hurried on. "Our librarian has been kind enough to do some research for us, and has just sent over this nice report — " Mrs. Fellows waved a piece of paper, immediately dropped it, and stepped on it as she bent to pick it up. After smoothing out the wrinkles she read:

"The town of Mapleton was founded in 1722 by Silas Barrington. He was a pack peddler who traded with the Indians for a large tract of land running from the edge of the stream where Judson's farm now stands, clear across the valley. He built an inn close to the trail along which pioneers were traveling in great numbers, and sold parcels of land to the settlers. A town soon grew up around the inn, and Silas Barrington, who had become very wealthy, was the town's leading citizen. At that time the settlement was known as Barrington's Corners, but a short time later when Squire Barrington was caught in a dishonest land deal — " Mrs. Fellows' voice faltered. "There must be some mistake," she said. "We can't put that in the pageant, oh my! Well, anyway, Squire Barrington hastily moved out west — for his health, do you suppose, ladies? Yes, for his health, it must have been, but let's leave that part out. Anyway the name of the town was changed to Mapleton because of the beautiful trees that grew in the forest all around. And the town has been growing in beauty and industry ever since," she finished triumphantly, "for two hundred wonderful years!"

Everyone applauded loudly. Then Mrs. Daley got up on the platform to tell everyone what the pageant would be like. The little ones were getting pretty restless with all this talking going on, and there was a great deal of shuffling and wrestling over in that section. Mrs. Bryant was trying to keep order and she looked almost done in. It was hard to tell what Mrs. Daley was talking about, but it seemed that the pageant was to start by showing Silas Barrington trading with the Indians. Mrs. Daley looked at the long list in her hand and announced that Banker Hopkins would play the

91

part of Silas Barrington, Mr. George Hutchens and a number of others would be Indians, and Clancy Chapman would be Silas Barrington's son, Jeremiah.

When Clancy heard this, he felt that all hope had left him. If the Tigers were just nameless pioneer boys like Philip and Georgie and Smelly and the others, it might be possible to get out of it somehow without being missed. But if he had been given a name and a real part, then everyone would expect him to go through with it.

He was looking enviously at Bill and Scudder when he heard Mrs. Daley say, "The next scene shows a pioneer family building their cabin, the first to be finished in Mapleton. All the new settlers help, and when it is built they have a party. We'll have a fiddler — Jonathan Amory of the High School orchestra will play — and a gay dance in the clearing by all the pioneers, young and old."

Scudder seemed to gag slightly at this point, and Bill, too, looked ill. Clancy decided there were worse things than being Jeremiah Barrington — but not much worse.

Mrs. Daley had to clear her throat and raise her voice to be heard over the confusion. "Now let's everybody go right on being sweet and cooperative while we get this first scene ready. Indians, please — and Silas Barrington, will you bring your pack? And shouldn't Clancy be carrying something to trade with the Indians, too? Somebody give Clancy a bag or basket — and have we enough Indian blankets, Mrs. Fellows? Quiet, please, while we count blankets — "

The noise was terrific. Mrs. Bryant's young charges had gotten out of control again and were running around. Some of the blankets were missing, and when the Indian blankets were finally found, the Indians were missing.

Somebody had thrust a big covered basket into Clancy's unwilling hand, and he wandered around with it, not knowing what he was supposed to do. Bill and Scudder were just as confused.

"They're going to have to go some to get this mess into shape by the Fourth of July," said Scudder. "It's

going to be terrible even if they do it right, and it won't be right, not with us dancing."

"We'll get out of it, see if we don't," said Bill soothingly. "Clancy'll think of an idea."

Clancy wasn't so sure. He didn't have an idea in his head, good or bad. He wasn't even thinking when he put out his foot to trip Dodie Haines as she passed. It was just an automatic reaction — you see Dodie, you trip her, just like that. Dodie's reaction wasn't automatic, however. She was mad, though unhurt, as she picked herself off the floor.

"You — you old boy, you! You ought to be put out of this pageant! And you will, too, if I tell on you!"

Clancy knew better. He felt sure that no matter what the Tigers did, they wouldn't be put out of the pageant. Pioneer boys were too much in demand. Too bad, he thought, we don't have a chance. He reckoned without Mrs. Holloway, though.

Mrs. Holloway was late for the rehearsal. She came sailing into the Town Hall basement, full of apologies for her tardiness. As usual, she started immediately to boss things, even though it was nice Mrs. Daley who was supposed to be in charge.

"I'm soooo sorry to be late," she cried. "But I see you've all been working away like good little elves. Now, just let me get my gloves off, and we'll get some order out of this dreadful shambles."

Clancy could see by the dark glances that were

94

thrown her way that this didn't go down so well with some of the ladies.

"First things first," she said. "Let's begin with Silas Barrington and the Indians — Oh Lulu, dear," she broke off to say to Mrs. Farlow, "that costume will never, never do, so run along like a lamb and put on something more appropriate. Now for Silas and his son — "

Mr. Hopkins, the president of the bank, stepped forward and Clancy followed, rather sheepishly. Mrs. Holloway took one look at him and gasped,

"Oh no! Mrs. Daley, have you given the part of Jeremiah Barrington to this — this *Clarence Chapman?*"

At Mrs. Daley's nod she gasped again.

"Well! All I have to say is — I haven't a thing to say! But he'd better behave — no tricks, mind you, Clarence!"

Clancy, his ears flaming, swallowed hard. Mrs. Holloway hadn't forgotten or forgiven the turtle affair. And she wasn't going to let him forget it either.

Mrs. Holloway went on wtih her business of bossing the pageant. She watched Clancy like a hawk, and backed away suspiciously whenever he came near.

"What's he got in that basket?" she asked Mrs. Daley in a loud whisper, and did not seem at all relieved when Mrs. Daley assured her that the basket was empty. Bill and Scudder watched in silent sym-

95

pathy. They were in this mess, but Clancy was in even deeper with Mrs. Holloway on his neck.

Dodie and Pat and Dulcy weren't sympathetic at all. They thought it was terribly funny. While Clancy was standing at one side waiting for his turn to follow Mr. Hopkins across the platform, the girls crowded around him.

"What *do* you have in your basket, Clarence?"

He was mad as a hornet at being called Clarence, but it wouldn't do to let the girls know they had gotten his goat.

"Don't tell on me," he whispered. "Mrs. Holloway thinks it's empty."

They were interested, hoping to find something else to tease him about.

"Well, we had to find someplace to keep our pet garter snakes. They kept crawling out of our pockets — "

There was a shriek from the three girls, and all of a sudden Clancy was standing there by himself.

I didn't tell a lie, he thought cheerfully. I never said our snakes were in the basket. The dopey girls should remember that we turned those snakes loose last spring.

The next chance he had, Clancy sidled up to the girls and made a soft scratching noise on the bottom of the basket. They screeched again, and hurried over to stand close to Mrs. Daley and the rest of the pio-

96

neers. This was good, Clancy thought. He went back
up on the stage again, almost in a good humor for
the first time that afternoon. He really had those old
girls on the run.

Dulcy turned to Scudder and hissed, "Just wait
till I get you home — you and your reptiles!"

Scudder asked wide-eyed, "What reptiles? But
Dulcy continued, "Don't give me that innocent look!
You know perfectly well what I'm talking about — and
you too, Bill Brown!"

Dodie was indignant, too.

"Of all the things to bring to a rehearsal! I'm sur-

prised you had sense enough to put them in the basket. It'd be just like you Tigers to let snakes run around all over the floor!"

Scudder was honestly surprised. "What basket? What snakes?"

Mrs. Daley turned then and hushed them up. "Don't interrupt Clancy's speech," she whispered. "He's doing awfully well. He's really getting in the spirit of the thing."

Mrs. Holloway didn't think so. She had a flock of pointed remarks to make about Clancy's performance, but he hardly noticed. He couldn't wait for his next chance to scratch the basket and worry the girls.

He got his chance all right, but he hadn't counted on Emily Allen. Dodie must have told her about the basket, for as Clancy came up behind her and scratched, she whirled around and hollered at the top of her lungs, "You get away from me, Clancy Chapman! Take that basket out of here!"

The big room was suddenly quiet. Everyone stopped to listen. Emily went right on yelling. Mrs. Holloway came down from the stage and asked coldly, "What is this disgraceful shouting about?"

Emily was too excited to care what Mrs. Holloway thought. She kept giving out shrill squeaky eeeeeeeee's and pointing at the basket.

"Snakes! The basket's full of snakes!"

There was a screech that put Emily's to shame, and

with one wild leap Mrs. Holloway scrambled up on the stage. She stood there, gibbering and pointing at Clancy and screaming,

"Out! Put him out! Get those snakes out of here!"

Clancy struggled with the lid of the basket.

"Honest, Mrs. Holloway, there's nothing in the basket! I'll show you — "

But she yelled again, "No, NO! Keep that lid on, and get out of here!"

Bill and Scudder weren't sure what was going on, but they felt they had to try to help Clancy out of his trouble.

"There aren't any snakes here," they said together, and Bill added, "We don't even have snakes any more."

"There!" Mrs. Holloway shrieked. "They've admitted they have snakes! You're out of the pageant, all three of you! Go, this very minute!"

"But — I — " protested Clancy. Scudder and Bill, one on each side of him, took him by the arm.

"You heard the lady," said Scudder firmly. "We're out of the pageant, *all three of us.* Don't argue."

The room was buzzing again. Mrs. Daley was saying over and over that she didn't believe it, that she'd never find three more pioneers at this late date, and what was she to do?

As they passed young Mrs. Bryant, she looked at them enviously.

"How'd you do it, boys?" she inquired.

"I don't know," answered Clancy, still dazed. "It all happened so fast — "

She shook her head sadly. "Some people have all the luck," she said.

IT HAD been a long hot day and a long hot night and from the looks of things there was another hot day coming up. In his little room under the roof Clancy twisted and turned and lay miserably perspiring on the wrinkled mess he had made of his bed.

Usually he fell asleep almost as soon as his head hit the pillow, but the sun that blazed down all day had made an oven of his room, and not a breath of cool air found its way to his window.

At last he could stand it no longer. With a final punch at his pillow that sent it off the bed onto the floor, he got up and leaned out the window, hoping for a breeze. But Mapleton's maples — usually stirring with the wind that blew across the valley, carrying smells of cool woods and fragrant hay fields — tonight the maples were still. Not a leaf turned, no faint sleepy tree frog chirped. The hot, heavy air pressed down on the town. Far away there was an occasional flash of heat lightning, but it was too far away for any hope of relief.

Clancy leaned on his elbows and sighed. Somehow a mosquito had got in and that added the final touch to his misery. It buzzed and he slapped and felt even warmer for the useless exertion. He looked longingly at the sky for a sign that it was growing lighter, that soon it would be morning. But dawn was hours away, and after awhile he made a halfhearted attempt to smooth out his sheet, and lay down again.

He slept at last, but woke very early feeling cranky and out of sorts. For once Grandma wasn't up when he came down to the kitchen. He could have fixed his own breakfast, of course, but he couldn't think of anything that appealed to him. So he wandered out to the front walk to swing listlessly on the gate and stare at the empty street.

At last he saw someone coming along. It was Mr. Jones, the school principal, taking his old dog Melinda out for her morning walk. The small-town dogs of Mapleton usually took their own walks, running free and visiting favorite trees and posts with groups of friends. But Melinda was really old — old and fat and forgetful. She had been known to wander away and had been brought home by the milkman or the mailman who found her blocks from home, plodding along in the middle of the street.

So Mr. Jones walked her faithfully morning and evening. He was pleased to see Clancy. Dog-walking can be very dull, especially with a slow old dog like Melinda.

"Hello, there, Clancy," he said. "How are things going with you?"

Clancy answered warily, hoping that perhaps Mr. Jones had forgotten that business of the Maypole.

"Oh, fine," he said. "Just dandy."

"That's not what I've been hearing," said Mr. Jones. "Heard the other day that you Tigers got thrown out of the Fourth of July pageant for some sort of monkey business. That doesn't fit in with the bargain you fellows made with me on the last day of school, you know. Better give it some serious thought."

Clancy didn't know what to say. He squirmed a little and tried to think of a reasonable answer. Before he could get his tired brain working Melinda yipped and pulled on her leash. This was a sign that she wanted to move on, and Mr. Jones dutifully followed her, waving goodbye with his free hand.

"Remember, serious thought," he called back.

Serious thought was the last thing Clancy felt up to that morning. He really didn't feel up to anything. And when Grandma called sharply, "Clancy! Clancy, where are you? Come here this minute," he groaned and started for the kitchen.

Apparently Grandma hadn't slept very well, either. She was often brisk or firm, but hardly ever irritable.

This morning, though, she was downright mad, and with good reason. One of the chores that had been assigned to Clancy when he came to stay was the job of emptying the icebox pan.

As the cake of ice that Grandma bought each day melted down, the water ran through a drain in the bottom of the big oak icebox and into a pan beneath it. The pan *had* to be emptied every night at bedtime or by morning it would overflow on the kitchen floor. And that is just what had happened. There was a puddle all around the icebox and Grandma was on her knees mopping frantically.

"Well, young man," she snapped. "Fine mess we have here. Don't just stand there — get a mop from the shed and help me! No, not the dry mop — the wet mop! The one with the strings."

He finally found the right tool and swished and sloshed away until the puddle was dry. Then Grandma decided that as long as he had gone that far he might as well mop the whole floor while she started breakfast.

"Too hot to heat up the stove," she said. "We'll have shredded wheat and huckleberries."

Even that seemed too much for Clancy, but he didn't dare say no. It just wasn't the morning for saying no to Grandma.

The field mice had had a difficult night, too, it appeared, for instead of his usual one or two, Jelly had left an offering of three mice on the doorstep. Getting rid of them was one more unpleasant job for Clancy.

Breakfast was hardly a relaxing meal. Grandma gave him a good stiff lecture about shirking responsibility, and forgetfulness, and spending his time in wasteful idleness — and this, on top of Mr. Jones's warning, made him feel lower than a gopher hole. Then somehow Grandma got off on the subject of the Fourth of July Celebration and how the Tigers didn't even have enough get-up-and-go to take an interest —

Suddenly the cuckoo hiccuped, the door flew open and the little wooden bird cuckooed eight times. Grandma looked up in amazement.

"Eight o'clock! Clancy, I'm ashamed of myself. I've been jawing away at you for a full hour, and all because a ding-donged mosquito kept me awake half the night. I'm sorry, I honestly am."

Grandma looked so unhappy that Clancy couldn't stay cross.

"I did forget the icebox pan," he reminded her. "I can't blame that on the mosquitoes or the heat."

"Well, what's done is done, and the floor got a good scrubbing with ice water. Probably the coolest floor in Mapleton, and that's something on a day like this."

She thought for a moment as she put their cereal bowls in the sink and ran the water.

"Why don't you boys go up to Horsetail for the day? Just sit in the water and soak and keep cool, even if it isn't deep enough for swimming. It would be better than sitting around here sweltering all day. Round up the other two, and by the time you get back I'll have a lunch packed for all of you."

Grandma always said that grandparents and great-grandparents had a big advantage over parents, especially where boys were concerned. After all she said, we're not responsible for a child's manners or bringing up, and we don't have to sign report cards or try to keep him clean and kind to animals. So we can just lean back and enjoy him and let his mother and father do the worrying. Usually this was what she did, just leaned back and enjoyed her great-grandson. And if in

106

the process of enjoying him, she taught him a lot about manners and cleanliness and kindness and courage, it was something that neither of them noticed because they were having such a good time.

Once the air was cleared between them and they were back on their usual easy footing, both of them felt much better. Grandma hummed as she started to pack the picnic lunch and Clancy raced through his morning chores in no time flat. Then he biked off to find Bill and Scudder and helped them with their chores to speed things up as much as possible. Before long the Tigers were on Grandma's back steps, ready to go.

It was hot at Horsetail Creek, too. It was hot everywhere. But the creek water was cool, and with a little searching they found a pool deep enough to come up to their chins when they were sitting on the bottom.

"If only there was a place around here to swim," Scudder complained. "That's the only thing wrong with Mapleton. No lake, no pond — only this shallow little creek."

Bill paddled his hands and poured some water over his head.

"What we need is an engineering project," he said. "We should build a dam. Then we'd have a place to swim."

Scudder suggested, "What we need is a troop of trained beavers. We'd point to the right trees and

107

they'd chaw them down and build the dam exactly where we need it."

"Always the easy way out for Scudder." Bill knew Scudder pretty well. "By the time you got your beavers trained, Clancy and I could have a dam built and be swimming."

Scudder still didn't take the idea seriously. "All right," he said. "That's a deal. I'll start lining up my beavers, and you and Clancy start hauling rocks, and then if I find I've made a mistake and my plan won't work, I'll swallow my pride and swim in your lake."

"A pond sure would be more fun than just sitting here," said Clancy. "Are you serious, Bill? Is there enough water trickling down this little creek to make a worthwhile pond?"

"Sure. Down below there where the creek widens out near the sheep meadow. If we took the stones out of the creek bed and piled them up, the water would back up between the banks — not deep, maybe, but swimmable. If Mr. Judson would let us, that is. We'd have to ask him first."

Scudder scrambled to his feet.

"What are we sitting around here for," he yelled. "Come on, let's find Mr. Judson and ask him."

They finally found Mr. Judson in the big hay barn. He listened patiently to their plan as they explained excitedly what they had in mind.

"Mighty hot day for all that rock piling," he said.

"But if you want to try it, it's O.K. with me. Only one stipulation, though. If you get a place deep enough for a dip, you've got to let me come in too, once my chores are done."

Grinning, they promised, and hurried back to the creek. They let Bill take charge of the planning since he was considered the engineer of the group. He chose the best place to build the dam and they started to work.

It was one of those jobs that looked easier than it actually was. The small stones in the creek bed were easy to move, but the pile they made grew in an exasperatingly slow way. The bigger rocks were firmly embedded and did not yield to all their tugging. Just about the time that they had begun to wonder if perhaps Scudder's idea had been the simpler one, they heard voices from the woods at the top of the hill.

"Duck," said Scudder. "Maybe it's the girls." But it wasn't. Georgie Mears and Philip Higgins and Smelly Schmell came down across the field.

"Hi!" they shouted, and were amazed at the enormously enthusiastic greeting they got from the Tigers.

"Well, well," said Clancy, slapping Smelly on the back. "We were just wondering if you fellows were coming to cool off in the pond."

"Yeah," added Scudder, "we kept thinking too bad old Phil and old Georgie and old Smell aren't here to enjoy a dip in the pond."

"Pond?" Georgie was suspicious. "I don't see no pond."

"Of course not, not right this minute." Bill was hearty. "Just give us a hand with this rock here and before you know it, we'll be in over our heads, yessir. Just grab this little old rock here —"

Before they knew it, the newcomers were hauling rocks, too, urged on by the loud admiration of the Tigers.

"Boy, look at old Phil lift. He's really got a set of muscles on him." And old Phil lifted. A fellow with a set of muscles could do no less.

Six extra hands made the work go much faster. Before long there was a stone wall from one bank of the creek to the other. Not a neat wall nor a straight one, and water ran through every chink. But it was enough of a dam to hold back a good part of the creek. By the time Mrs. Judson rang the noon dinner bell at the farmhouse, it was plain that the dam was going to work.

"We've gotta go home," said Georgie. "But we'll be right back, soon as we eat."

"My grandma packed a lunch for three. That means there'll be more than enough for six. So stay and we'll watch the pond fill up while we eat."

The six boys stretched out on the creek bank to eat their lunch. Clancy divided everything into six piles, even breaking cookies in half to make them come out

110

right. Just as he had predicted, there was plenty to
go around. They didn't talk much, just munched away
and watched the water back up behind their little dam.
The water level rose gradually until it came almost to

the top of the bank — a good five feet deep and fine for swimming.

They were frantic to try it, but Bill was firm. "Not for an hour after we've eaten," he proclaimed. "When Mr. Judson and his hired man go out the back door — that's an hour. That's how long Mr. Judson always takes off."

Because Bill was acknowledged to be the best informed in scientific matters, they followed his direction. At the sound of the squeak of the back screen door they were ready to jump in, but it was only Mrs. Judson coming out to toss her soapy dishwater on the rose bushes.

The next squeak, though, was Mr. Judson and Si, and with a wild yell, the six boys leaped into their new little lake. The rest of the afternoon was pure heaven. It was not a perfect lake, by any means. The bottom was rocky in places and full of holes in others, and it was so small that six splashing boys filled it almost to the limit. But they gladly made room for Mr. Judson and Si when they had finished their hot work in the barn.

"By golly, I hate to get out," Si said when the dinner bell rang again.

"By golly," said Clancy, "we'd better get out or we'll get skinned alive. I should have been home an hour ago."

They were so waterlogged that their hands and feet

were all puckered, and every nose was sunburned bright red.

"This has been a real Tiger of a day," Scudder said, forgetting that only three of them were Tigers.

Smelly, his voice muffled by the shirt that he was pulling over his head, said, "I guess it's pretty good, being a Tiger. Seems like you Tigers have all the nifty times." And Georgie added wistfully, "I don't suppose you ever take in any new members, do you?"

Clancy and Scudder and Bill looked at each other. Why not? It had been fun, having extra help with the work, and there were a lot of projects they could try if they had six Tigers instead of three.

Then Clancy remembered Mr. Jones's warning only that morning. By fall there might not be a Tigers Club at all.

"Oh, I don't know," he said, keeping his voice unconcerned. "We just might, come end of summer. We'd have to have a Board of Directors meeting to consider it. We could let you know, if you'd be interested."

The day had been such a good one that they hated to have it end.

"Goodbye," they called as one after the other peeled off and turned in at his own gate. Grandma was waiting on the front porch watching the Tigers come up the street.

"About time you three showed up," she said. "An-

113

other few minutes and I'd have started to worry. Check in with your families, Scudder and Bill, and if you want, you can come back here for supper. I've set the table on the back porch where it's cool."

The boys did want, and they set off at a run to get permission to stay at Grandma's for supper.

"Don't tell the girls," warned Clancy as Scudder hurried away. He called back, "What do you think I am, a stupe or something? That pond is ours!"

They told Grandma all about the day's adventures at supper time. After they had helped with the dishes, they sat on the front porch, too full and sleepy to do anything more energetic.

It was hot again but they were too contented to mind. Grandma fanned gently with her palm-leaf fan as she rocked. Occasionally there was a flash of heat lightning and Bill said he thought it might rain. Scudder said there had been heat lightning and even thunder the night before and it hadn't amounted to anything. And anyway, the weatherman didn't predict rain until Saturday.

After a series of long, lazy silences, Bill finally said that he thought it was time to go home, and he'd probably sleep like a log. Scudder said he was half asleep already, and didn't think he had the strength to make it around the corner to his house.

So Clancy said, "Stay here. We can sleep outside in the backyard and keep cool."

"It sure would beat sleeping inside," said Bill. "Our bedroom was as hot as a cookstove and Buggy moaned and lashed around the whole night long."

Scudder suddenly found the strength to go home and ask permission to sleep at Clancy's, and in a very short time he and Bill were both back with old blankets, half a chocolate cake left from the Browns' supper, and a plate of deviled eggs from Mrs. Williams. She also sent word that Scudder must report back to his family at least once every three years or he would lose his citizenship rights and would belong to Grandma Chapman permanently.

Grandma had several rather ripe bananas and some big dill pickles, and she felt this small snack should hold them until morning — if their outdoor sleep lasted that long.

"First mosquito that comes zooming around will drive you in," she prophesied, "but if you do come in, there's always the porch. It's screened."

They folded their blankets to make as thick a mattress as possible, but even so, the hard ground seemed mighty hard and lumpy. But it was cool. A breeze had come in from somewhere, somewhere else where it was raining, perhaps, and it was very pleasant. They had arranged their beds with the heads all pointed in together, with a circle in the center just large enough to hold the tray of snacks. That way each boy had only to reach his hand over his head, feel around in the darkness for a pickle or a piece of cake, and go off to sleep with no fear of starvation before morning.

Each flash of lightning flared brighter and oftener, accompanied now by a low growl of distant thunder. But the Tigers had fallen asleep. The sting of mosquito bites, the heat from their sunburned shoulders, their hard beds, the rising wind — nothing could make them stir. Not even the bananas and pickles disturbed their heavy breathing.

Not until the storm actually broke did they waken. At the first big drops Clancy woke, grabbed his blanket, shouted to the others and headed for the house. The rain was really dumping down by the time they reached the porch. Upstairs, Clancy heard windows being slammed down, and he hurried to close the windows in the kitchen and settin' room before anything got soaked.

The Tigers thought they could put their blankets on the porch floor and settle down again, but Grandma and the driving rain changed their minds.

"The porch is half soaked already," Grandma said, "and if this wind keeps up there won't be a dry spot on it. Shove the furniture around in the settin' room and you'll have a rug under you to make your beds a little softer."

She turned on the light switch, but the room remained dark. "Lines are down somewhere. I'll fetch an oil lamp from the kitchen."

116

The boys insisted they didn't need a light, and really, the flashes of lightning were so bright and so close together that they could easily see to make room for their floor beds. They moved the fancy carved chairs

back against the wall, and made sure the what-not with the birds'-eggs and the shells was out out of the way. In a few minutes each was bedded down again.

"I hate to admit it, being a great outdoor man," said Scudder, "but a rug makes a better foundation than that lumpy backyard."

"And it's not quite so buggy," Clancy agreed.

They all jumped as a flash of lightning and a clap of thunder roared right overhead.

"It's not particularly quiet in here, though," Bill added drowsily. "It's almost noisy enough to keep me awake."

Scudder was determined not to let anything interfere with his night's sleep, and he pulled part of his blanket over his head and turned toward the wall. In a few minutes, Clancy could hear his even breathing. Bill tossed a little longer, but soon he too gave in and went to sleep.

Clancy felt all slept out. He lay there listening to the wind lash the tall trees above the house, and was grateful for the lightning rod on the cupola. There would be a lot of lawn-raking tomorrow — branches and leaves all over the place. And Grandma's gladiolas would be knocked flat. He wondered about their dam. Would the sudden rush of water in Horsetail carry the dam away? If it did, they'd build it up again, the Tigers and Phil and Georgie and Smelly.

Twice the thunder died away in the distance and twice it came back again, but with lessening vigor each time. At last it rumbled and bumbled away and Mapleton was quiet.

Still Clancy couldn't sleep. The room was stuffy and close now that the rain had stopped. Scudder moaned. Too much late eating, most likely. Pickles and chocolate cake. Bill turned over and bumped the organ pedal. The organ gave a dusty sigh of protest and was still again.

Clancy gathered up his blanket, stepped high over the lump that was Scudder and tiptoed to the front door. It opened with a faint jangle of the old crank-type doorbell. Try as he might he could never get the door open without making at least a small sound. No one stirred, and he went out onto the rain-soaked porch. The air was cool and fresh and sweet-smelling. Patches of ragged clouds were blowing past the moon.

It'll be nice tomorrow, he thought. The swing seat was damp but it wouldn't soak through his blanket. It was a nice feeling, being the only one in the house awake. Maybe somewhere in another house someone was wide awake and listening to the night sounds of Mapleton. But Clancy felt as if he alone in all the town heard a dog bark at the newly washed moon. He heard the leaves rustle, and the small sound that was rainwater running down the gutter into the storm sewer at the corner. Hanscom's gate, the one with the broken latch that Mr. Hanscom was always promising to fix, banged. Something black and fast streaked across the yard. Probably Jelly, up to no good.

There was the funny grinding sound that meant the cuckoo clock was going to strike. The little bird hiccuped, the door flew open and the cuckoo called four times from the kitchen. Four o'clock. Clancy yawned and rolled up in his blanket. It had been a long day.

8

THE NEXT few days were busy ones for Clancy, but uneventful. There was Grandma's lawn and garden to take care of. Then he made a trip up the hill to his own house, where the lawn was beginning to be long and shaggy. He mowed the grass, weeded and watered the flower beds. He read his daily letters from his parents and wrote them a long letter telling them all about the pageant and the Tigers' unexpected release.

And every spare minute he was thinking, thinking, thinking. He was thinking hard about a plan to win the prize at the Celebration, for the time was growing very short.

At one of the Tigers Club meetings he said determinedly that something had to be decided soon. The

Tigers were having the meeting, informally as usual, out in Grandma's backyard. Scudder rolled over on the grass and looked up at the sky.

"I'm all for action," he said, "I never was any good at thinking. But what action shall we do?"

Bill said mournfully, "This is the first time the Tigers haven't been able to come up with *something*." There was silence again, and then after a while, Bill said enthusiastically, "I have it! Let's build a great big firecracker in the front yard and shoot it! I don't suppose we could get any gunpowder, but we'll do it with a steam boiler and a big fire —"

Clancy pointed out that Horace would have to approve first, and that took care of their idea. They went back to their serious thinking. Bill was still simmering with what he considered wonderful plans, forgetting that some of his wonderful plans with chemistry had gotten the Tigers into trouble in the past. When he was reminded of this, he regretfully put those ideas out of his mind and turned his thoughts in another direction.

"Music is always good. We can have a hidden orchestra. We'll climb up in the tree and hide and serenade the judges and surprise them with all sorts of patriotic songs —"

Scudder was the wet blanket for that one.

"There are only three of us, and Clancy's the only one who can play a mouth organ fit to be heard. Not much of an orchestra. Come on, Bill, you're the thinker in the club, you'll have to do better than that."

But Bill's inspirations had petered out, and they were right back where they started from.

Wonderful smells were drifting out from the kitchen. Grandma was baking cake, cookies, and a big apple pie. Scudder sniffed appreciatively as Grandma came to the door and said, "First batch of cookies will be out in a minute. Don't go away."

While they were waiting, Clancy said, "Maybe Horace Henderson will help us think of something that will win the prize. We certainly don't seem to be able to do it."

Grandma called them, then, and the Tigers made short work of a plate of oatmeal cookies as she watched admiringly.

"Nothing does me so much good as to see a bunch of boys eat cookies," she said. "No waste motions or fooling around. Pure efficiency, that's what it is. I guess your experience as play-actors didn't hurt your appetite any."

"It sharpened mine," said Scudder solemnly. "I've eaten like a horse ever since, just as if I'd been let out of prison."

"Where to now, boys?" asked Grandma as they scooped up the last crumbs of cookies.

"We thought we'd mosey over and chew the fat with Horace for a while," answered Clancy vaguely. "We've got some problems to talk over."

But Horace, for once, wasn't very helpful. He pushed back his hat and scratched his head when the boys told him what they wanted to do.

"MMMMmmm —" he drawled, sitting down in the shade to rest. "Winning the Celebration prize is a good idea, all right. That should fix you up fine with Mr. Jones. But I can't think of anything for you to do — not right offhand, I can't. If you get an idea, better check with me before you go too far. Some of your plans are a mite wild, you know."

The boys were discouraged. They had counted on Horace, and here he didn't have any brilliant ideas either. There was nothing to do but go back to Grandma's and eat some more cookies.

As they came moping along the street they saw that something was going on at Grandma's house. Grandma and her next-door neighbor, Mrs. Hanscom, were out in the yard looking at something up on the roof. Little Ruthie Hanscom was there too, bawling her head off, and pointing. There was an assortment of other children, three- and four-year-old friends of Ruthie, all yelling, "Come down, kitty! Here kitty, kitty, kitty!"

"Ruthie's kitten followed Peanut Butter up on the roof," explained Grandma, "and now it's scared to come down. You boys climb up and catch it, will you?"

The Tigers were pleased to have something to do.

They scrambled up the apple tree and out onto the big branch that overhung the low porch roof. Then a quick climb to the topmost gable where the trembling black kitten clung to the peak and meowed. Peanut Butter had moved from the roof to the top of the tree when all the excitement began, and he watched the proceedings with a kind of lazy scorn. He had forgotten his once-foolish kitten days, it seemed.

"Nice kitty, nice kitty," said Clancy soothingly. "Come on, kitty, let go — ouch!" The kitten let go of the roof and clung just as hard to Clancy's hand.

"Ouch!" he yelled again. "Let go, you little black imp!"

"What's the matter?" jeered Bill. "Has a little tiny kitten got you buffaloed?"

"You take it then, smarty." And Bill found himself with a clawing bunch of fur in his surprised hands.

"Hold on," yelled Scudder. "I'll fix him!"

He stripped off his shirt and wrapped it around the struggling kitten. Then with the bundle under his arm, he swung from roof to the branch, and down the tree to the ground.

When Ruthie had her kitten back and Mrs. Hanscom had called her thanks to the boys, Grandma said, "Well, that bit of excitement calls for a snack all around. More cookies?"

"Let's eat ours up here," said Clancy. "Bring 'em up, Scudder. And bring up the first-aid kit, too. That little kitten put up a real fight."

Bill and Clancy leaned back against the cupola and waited for the refreshments to be brought up to them. Bill looked around at the fancy wooden cutouts that decorated the cupola.

"Why do they call this stuff gingerbread?" he asked

126

lazily. "Looks more like the trimming on a wedding cake to me — or a birthday cake."

"Yeah," agreed Clancy. "This whole house is like a big birthday cake — "

His voice faded away. Somewhere in the back of his mind, a bell rang, a light flashed on, the Big Idea was forming . . . Scudder clambered up on the roof with a big bag of cookies just as Clancy said excitedly, "I think maybe I got it! I think — now don't get into a tizzy," he said as Scudder and Bill broke into happy grins. "Maybe it's not so good. We'll have to figure it out."

"Well, don't be mysterious, tell us!" demanded Bill.

"When you said birthday cake, it struck me. Why can't we fix up this house to represent a big birthday cake, with lights on it like candles, and a big banner across the front saying Happy Birthday, Mapleton, or something like that?"

Scudder and Bill were wildly enthusiastic. They were sure that Clancy's idea was a prizewinner, and they wanted to get to work on it right away.

"How will we get the lights up on the roof without Grandma knowing?"

"We'll cross that bridge when we come to it. First, let's see about getting the lights. We really should have two hundred of them, but we'll probably have to settle for less. Maybe the number won't matter so much, just as long as we can get the house to look like a cake to the judges." Right after the lunch dishes were washed, they hurried down to the hardware store. It was a fascinating place, and usually they lingered over the tools and fishing tackle, but today they got right down to business.

"We need a whole lot of those electric lights that look like candles," explained Clancy. "You know, the kind people put in their windows at Christmas time."

Mr. Berry nodded. "I know what you mean. I might have a box, maybe two, left over from last Christmas, but they're all put away down in the basement. They come six to a box — would twelve be enough for you? A dollar seventy-nine a box, as I recall."

"We'd need an awful lot of them, a couple of hundred — did you say a dollar seventy-nine for *six?*"

The Tigers did some rapid mental calculations. Bill gasped, "Why we'd need fifty or sixty dollars' worth! We've only got four or five dollars between us!"

"Suppose we only got a few — no, that wouldn't look like anything at all. Unless we have enough to really make a show we'd better forget the whole idea. We just can't afford it."

Mr. Berry could see that they were disturbed and disappointed.

"Even if you had fifty or sixty dollars, boys, I don't have that many candle lights, and it would take me weeks and weeks to get the order through this time of year. I have lots of regular wax candles in stock, though, and they're cheap. Would they do?"

Would they? The Tigers thought it over. They were pretty sure that Horace wouldn't let them use lighted candles on the roof of Grandma's house, and yet — real candles would be perfect, flickering and sparkling. It would make the gingerbready little house just right —

"We'll have to talk it over, Mr. Berry. We'll be back later if we find out it's all right," said Clancy.

He was already turning over in his mind the arguments he could use to convince Horace that lighted candles would be safe. Scudder was downcast, sure that their wonderful plan would have to be dropped, but Bill was still hopeful. He said, "After all, Horace said he would help us any way he could. I think he'll be agreeable if we can just figure out a way to fasten the candles to the roof so they won't tip over and set fire to the shingles."

Clancy remembered something. "The shingles are fireproof, I'm pretty sure. Grandma had a new roof put on last year, and I remember Dad insisted she should have the kind that wouldn't burn."

"Well," said Scudder excitedly, beginning to think that the plan might work after all, "why can't we set the candles on fireproof strips, somehow — fasten them tight so they won't tip, and then lay the strips on the edge of the roof?"

Scudder, who claimed to be better at acting than thinking, was thinking very well. He went on, "We've got some of those fireproof shingles in our garage, left over from our roof, and we'll get some candles and try this out. Then when we go to see Horace we'll be able to show him that it really is safe."

They raced over to Scudder's garage, so excitedly that they forgot to be cautious. But luck was with them and none of Scudder's sisters noticed them. They were able to try out their scheme in secrecy. Scudder explained what he had in mind and then left Bill and Clancy to drive nails through the shingles, while he went in to ask his mother for some old stubs of candles. He was back in a minute with a handful of candle ends. Mrs. Williams had given him the candles with the warning that they were not to light them, absolutely, positively not. So they decided to get everything ready and let Horace do the lighting.

On each end of the long nails that had been driven

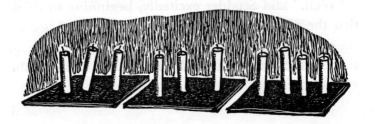

through the shingles, Scudder impaled a candle stub. It wasn't easy to make the candle stand up perfectly straight, and he split several before he finally got the hang of it.

At last he said proudly, "There. They won't tip, and even if one of them should fall over, it'd be resting on the shingle, see?"

It did, indeed, seem like a splendid solution to the problem. But they still had to convince Horace, and Horace wasn't easy to convince. At first his answer was a flat, "Nothing doing!"

"But Horace, look now —"

"Nothing doing," he said again. "That'd be a fine way to celebrate the town's birthday — set fire to the house of the Guest of Honor. And if I know anything about the Volunteers, they'll have the fire engine so decked out with flags and bunting that they couldn't put out a fire in a wastebasket. I'm sorry, boys, we just can't risk it. It's a grand idea, but it's not safe."

"Please, Horace, just listen to the way we've got it all worked out. It'd be safe, honest. At least give us a chance to explain before you say no," pleaded Clancy.

Horace was a fair man, so he waited patiently while they explained their scheme, how the candles couldn't possibly be a fire hazard if they were firmly fastened to the fireproof shingles and then set carefully on the fireproof roof.

When they had finished, he wrinkled his forehead

131

and thought about it for quite a while. At last he said, "We-e-ll, you fellows are mighty convincing. I don't see myself how any trouble could start. One thing, though, you'll have to let me examine every single candle and make sure it is standing upright before I put it up on the roof. And nobody but me is going to set a match to them, understand? And if it should come up windy on the Fourth of July, and I think there's any danger, I can call the whole thing off. Right?"

Horace and the delighted Tigers shook hands on the agreement. They could go ahead!

"I'll say this for you, boys, if your plan works out, it'll be a knockout. Nobody else in town will think of anything like this, I'll bet."

Now that their plan had been approved, there was a lot to do. They clambered all over the roof, measuring and deciding where the two hundred candles should go to make a really showy effect. They emptied their banks and poled their funds, four dollars and eighty-three cents.

Scudder's father said sure they could have that box of old shingles out in the garage, and what did they want them for anyway? When they said, Oh, just for messin' around with, he laughed and said he was glad to get the garage cleaned out and what about straightening out the toolbox while they were at it.

Since the shingles were free, they could spend all their money on candles. But even so, they still didn't have enough. They wanted two hundred, and the cheapest ones Mr. Berry had in stock were a nickel apiece. That made ten dollars they needed, and not much time left.

"I could borrow on next week's allowance," figured Bill, "but that would be only twenty cents more, and Dad won't let me get more than one week in debt."

"Tell you what," said Mr. Berry. "Since this seems to be an emergency, and you need the money bad, how about working out the difference? I can use some help around the store."

"Salesman?" asked Scudder, eagerly. "I could demonstrate the fishing tackle fine!"

"Nothing so fancy as that, I'm afraid. More like sweeping up, and opening boxes and bringing up stock from the basement. Do you want the job?"

Scudder looked slightly crestfallen that he would not be a star salesman, but he was as eager as the other two to earn the money they needed.

For the next few days they were really busy. Grandma complained that she never saw Clancy except at mealtimes, and then not for long. When they weren't needed at the hardware store they were at Bill's house, making the big banner that was to be draped across the front of the house.

They collected old sheets from Mrs. Williams and Mrs. Brown, and tore them into wide strips. Then they sewed the strips together until they had a piece of cloth about twenty-five feet long.

"That will be enough to go across the front of the house and hang down on each end, like this," said Clancy. He smoothed out a flat place in Buggy's sandbox and made a sketch in the sand.

"Then we paint on the big letters — sort of curly letters, like on a cake, you know, Happy Birthday Mapleton!"

"Will we have room for the dates, 1722–1922? That'd look neat, I think," said Bill.

"Sure, there'll be plenty of room. But first we've got to get these blooming pieces sewed together."

"How do girls do it so easy, I wonder?" Scudder was sucking a much-pricked thumb. "They sew right along and their fingers never seem to get in the way."

They had a lot of interruptions. Georgie and Philip came along and tried to get up a ball game, but for once the Tigers weren't interested. Georgie and Philip showed signs of wanting to hang around and talk, but were sent on their way rather abruptly.

"Whew! That was close. I was afraid they were going to ask what I was sitting on." Bill had gathered up the banner hastily when he heard the other boys calling, and was sitting firmly on the jumbled heap.

"Hope you didn't sit on a needle."

"It'll be the only place I haven't stuck myself," Bill grumbled as he went to work. "This sewing is a mess. There's something wrong with this thread, too. Keeps getting into knots. It'd be almost worth it to ask the girls to help us out."

"Not on your life!" Scudder exploded. "No girls on this project. This is one time we're going to do something without those pesky girls poking their noses into it. Ouch!" he added as he stuck his finger again.

"I hope your fingers hold out," said Clancy. He was struggling to thread his needle.

Scudder was firm. "I'll need a blood transfusion

135

when this is over, I've lost so much blood. But I don't care. We won't let anybody help us on this plan — except Horace, and he isn't exactly helping, just supervising. Remember Mr. Jones said we had to do it ourselves? We're on our own."

9

"Two hundred is a lot of candles," said Scudder. "I wouldn't have believed we could work so hard for so long on this job."

"Cheer up, Scud. We're almost done. Oh gosh! I split another one. We're going to run short, I'm afraid. I've busted an awful lot, trying to get them to stand up straight."

It was discouraging work. But they knew they had to keep trying, for Horace would insist that every candle be just right — or else!

"You know," said Clancy thoughtfully, as he hammered nails through the shingles, "we'll have to do some planning. If we get the candles lit too soon, they'll be burnt down before the judges come along. And if we wait too long to light them, it'll be just as bad."

The Tigers thought this over. At last they decided that what they needed was a schedule of the Fourth of July events. That way, they would be able to figure out just how much time they had between the supper at the Fire House and the judging, exactly how much time they had to get ready.

"Do you suppose we'll have to miss the supper?" asked Scudder anxiously. "I hear it's going to be super-swell."

"Just about every woman in town is making something special. Mom says they've got over ten dozen pies promised, and cakes and cookies and baked ham, and beans and fried chicken and all kinds of pickles and potato salad —" Bill had to stop and swallow, it all sounded so good.

"I'd sure hate to miss it."

Clancy frowned. The idea of missing it didn't appeal to him, either. Then he brightened and said, "Say, I've got a pile of these shingles nailed, enough to keep you two busy for awhile. Suppose I scout around and try to get an idea about the time they've allowed for all the stuff — the supper and speeches and everything."

The other Tigers agreed, so Clancy hurried off on his bike to get some information.

It seemed as if everyone in town was busy, too busy to bother with Clancy. He tried to talk to Mr. Farlow at Farlow's Fancy Grocery, but the storekeeper was trying to wait on customers, answer the phone, fill orders, and at the same time, count out the boxes and boxes of paper napkins he was delivering to the Fire House.

"Seventy-nine, eighty, eighty-three, eighty-four —
no, I've made a mistake somewhere, — oh, that dratted
phone again! Yes, ma'am, I'll be with you in just a
moment, soon as I answer the phone —"

"I'll count the boxes for you," said Clancy helpfully.
Mr. Farlow was a good friend and he needed help.
So Clancy counted the boxes and piled them up in

neat stacks. Then he carried them across the square to the Fire House, making trip after trip.

"Gosh, I've been gone a long while, and I still don't know how much time we'll have."

Mr. Farlow was talking on the phone again, so Clancy waved goodbye and went on to the drugstore. Mr. Hadley was busy, too. He was donating paper cups for the supper, and again Clancy found himself helping almost before he realized it.

Mr. Hadley wiped his forehead when they had finished carrying the cups over to the Fire House and fixed two lemon phosphates.

"Sure is a warm one," he said, as they stood on the sidewalk sipping the drinks and looking up at the cloudless blue sky. "Looks like we'll have another nice day tomorrow for the Celebration. This'll be the biggest day Mapleton has ever seen, yessir!"

Clancy grasped the chance to ask questions before Mr. Hadley got to work again.

"How long is the supper going to take, Mr. Hadley? And what time are they going to have this judging for the prize?"

"Well, we're starting the supper at five o'clock so's we can get everybody fed by seven, we hope. As the first bunch finish eating, they're to go next door to the Town Hall. We'll have the orchestra playing for dancing in the basement, and plenty of chairs for those who're too stuffed to dance. Then at seven-fifteen or so everybody is to be at the Square for the speeches."

Clancy asked how long the speeches were expected to last.

"Not too long if I have anything to do with it, which I don't, unfortunately. The Mayor is going to talk, and then Senator White will make the main speech of the evening. Both of those boys tend to be pretty long-winded." He sighed, and wiped his perspiring forehead again. "There's nothing like a Fourth of July Celebration to bring out the orator in a man. The Senator will talk on until morning, but Ase Farlow has promised to stop him with a sledgehammer, if need be, if he runs on past seven-forty-five."

Clancy was noting all these facts on a scrap of paper he had found in his pocket.

"Then we form the motor parade," went on Mr. Hadley, "real slow, so the folks on foot can keep up with the judges. We drive around to all the places that are entered in the contest. Course everybody has fixed up their houses some, flags and all, but you'd be surprised how many have entered the contest. Some real snappy stunts and decorations, so I hear."

Mr. Hadley took a list out of his pocket and consulted it. "Can't wait to see what all these people are going to have."

Clancy was struck by a sudden thought. "Do you have to *enter* this contest? I thought the judges would just drive around and look."

"Well, we thought of that, Clancy, but then we were afraid we might slip up and miss somebody. I don't have to tell you what a fuss that would make. So we made up an entry blank, all official-like, and then we worked out a parade route. I'm Parade Marshal, so to speak. I ride with the Mayor," he said modestly.

"Mr. Hadley, is it too late to put another name on that list?" Clancy was worried.

"Oh goodness yes! We closed the entries yesterday. Route's all scheduled."

"But couldn't you — oh, Mr. Hadley, you've just got to add one more name! Oh golly, please!"

Clancy thought frantically of all the work the Tigers had put in already, all those candles, the banner, and most important, the worthwhile project that was to save the club and at the same time win the prize for Grandma Chapman. Mr. Hadley studied his map.

"Why, I guess we can stick you on here at the end, Clancy. The judges will be driving down Main Street back to the Square — yes, we'll just put you right here at the end of the trip."

He started to write on his list, C-L-A-N-C-

"Put it in Grandma's name, please, because it's her house, but don't say a word to her. Us Tigers are working on the plan, and we're going to win the prize and surprise Grandma."

Mr. Hadley chuckled. "Pretty sure of yourself, aren't you? You'll have to have a mighty good stunt to beat some of these. I hear Alice Holloway is planning a pip."

142

Clancy waved a hasty goodbye and pedaled back to Scudder's house. Bill and Scudder had long since fastened on all the candles. They were waiting for him impatiently.

"You certainly took long enough," complained Scudder. "Wait'll you hear what we just found out. Guess what Mrs. Holloway is going to do?"

"I thought everybody was supposed to keep the plans a secret," said Clancy.

"Oh, you know Mrs. Holloway," said Bill disgustedly. "She couldn't keep a secret if her life depended on it. She's so sure she's going to win, she's bragging about it all over town. She told Mrs. Williams this morning."

"She's going to have old-fashioned lanterns hanging in all her trees so her yard will be real light. Then she'll have her card club all dressed up in colonial costumes —"

"Poor Mr. Holloway is going to be wearing satin knee pants, and a wig!" interrupted Scudder.

"— and they'll dance the minuet on the lawn, and then —"

"They're going to have balloons, about a million of them, with 1722–1922 printed on them, and they'll give them out to everybody in the crowd."

"Wow!" Clancy was impressed. "Mrs. Holloway is going to be a hard one to beat."

Scudder was confident. "I figure all we have to do is

go up to her house just as the judges get there, carrying baskets. She'll scream and holler at the sight of us and it'll bust up the act."

Bill and Clancy laughed, but they said that this prize had to be won fair and square, or things would be even worse for the Tigers Club. Scudder remembered Mr. Jones, and agreed.

"People always like to get something for free — they'll go for those free balloons. What could we give away?" asked Clancy.

"Food," said Scudder promptly. "Everybody likes food, even better than balloons. I'm hungry right now myself, come to think of it," he added.

There was a long pause while they thought. Then Bill said, "Cake. We'll give out pieces of cake, as if the house was really a cake and we had just cut it, see?"

Clancy and Scudder saw. They slapped Bill on the back and yelled, "The boy genius! That's a swell idea! Perfect!" Then their enthusiasm cooled a little. "Where do we get enough cake for a big crowd? We're broke."

"We bake it," said Scudder. "It's easy."

"Have you ever baked a cake?" asked Clancy suspiciously.

"No, but I've seen it done plenty of times. And I heard my mother say that if you can read nowadays, you can cook, so —"

"So we can all read, can't we? Let's go."

They hurried in to get their baking done before lunch. Scudder seemed sure that it would be perfectly all right with his mother, and anyway, she wasn't anywhere around, so they went right ahead. In a few minutes they had assembled an awesome array of utensils and were reading the instructions in Mrs. Brown's cookbook.

"This is easy for fellows as smart as us," boasted Scudder. "I'll bet those dumb old girls will be flabbergasted when they see how we make out."

Flabbergasted was hardly the word. Horrified would have been more like it.

"Oh, Scudder!" wailed Dulcy when she happened into the kitchen for a drink of water. "What on earth! What are you Tigers doing? The floor is a mess — even the wall — and look at the ceiling! The ceiling!"

It took a lot of explaining to make Dulcy understand that they hadn't meant to do it, that the first cake went off fine, and it was only the second one that had splashed all over. Bill had lifted the eggbeater out of the mixing bowl while he was still turning the handle. A slight mistake, nothing serious, but it made the kitchen look bad, that was all.

"Pat and I cleaned this kitchen only yesterday," moaned Dulcy as she looked around. "Say, what's burning?"

Scudder raced to open the oven, but he was too late. The first cake, the one that had turned out so fine, was burned. Hopelessly ruined.

Nobody said anything for a long time. The Tigers were so disappointed at the collapse of their wonderful plan that they couldn't talk. At last Dulcy said, "What I can't understand is why you did this in the first place. Mother baked two lovely cakes this morning, one for the supper tomorrow night, and the other for us. All you had to do was ask for a piece if you were hungry."

"We didn't want to *eat* the old cakes," said Scudder dismally. "The way I feel now I don't want to see another cake as long as I live."

"If I know you, that feeling will pass away," was his sister's cold answer. "But if you weren't going to eat the cakes, what then?"

The Tigers stared at the floor.

"You'd just better tell me. You'll have to give Mother some sensible reason for this crazy stunt." There was no answer.

"Come on, tell," coaxed Dulcy. "If you need a cake for a real good reason, maybe I could help you. I'm a good baker, you know."

Clancy brightened and looked at the other two.

"Say, maybe she could help us. What do you think, fellows? The cake idea is good, I'm sure of that. It might even be the extra touch that will win us the prize."

Bill was easily convinced but Scudder objected.

"What about Mr. Jones? We're supposed to do this project all by ourselves."

Clancy was excited. "Let's ask Horace what he thinks. If he says it's O.K. to let Dulcy help us, we ought to do it. Come on."

The three Tigers started to rush out but Dulcy blocked the door. "Oh no you don't," she said firmly. "I don't know what this is all about, but I'm not letting all three of you go until this mess is cleaned up. You go, Clancy, and the other two can stay here as hostages until you get back."

Clancy had never pedaled faster. He rode to Horace's house and luckily he found his friend at home.

147

He panted out his question and waited anxiously for the answer. It took Horace forever to make up his mind. Then he said, "You know, I think this is a matter for Mr. Jones to decide. Let me call him."

When Horace came back from the phone his eyes were twinkling. Mr. Jones had listened to the whole story of the Tigers' plan to win the prize, and had agreed that it was indeed a worthwhile project. He also felt, said Horace, that if the Tigers needed Dulcy's help, it would be perfectly all right for her to help them. And he wished them the very best of luck.

With this news, Clancy hurried back to the Williams house where Scudder and Bill were meekly mopping the floor under Dulcy's stern direction. Clancy asked, "Can you keep a secret, Dulce? You wouldn't go blabbing it all over?"

Dulcy gave him a withering look. "Of course I can keep a secret. Now tell."

So they explained the whole thing to Dulcy — about Mr. Jones, and the candles and the banner, and then about the cakes. She got more excited as she listened.

"Why that's wonderful! Really brainy! We'll win the prize for sure!"

"We?"

"Of course, we. I'm in it now, and we'll get Pat and Lou-Ann and Dodie and Emily to help, too."

There was a howl of anguish from the Tigers, but Dulcy was firm.

148

"Now don't you boys be ridiculous. We'll need dozens and dozens and *dozens* of tiny cupcakes to give away — cupcakes will be better than trying to hand out pieces of cake, we won't need plates — and if you think I can make that many cupcakes all by myself, you're crazy. We'll start right after lunch and if we work hard we can have them all made and iced by tomorrow."

They could see that Dulcy was right, and since they had failed so spectacularly at cake-baking, there was really nothing they could do about it. The other girls would have to be told.

In fact, once they got used to the idea, they were relieved to have that part of the job taken off their hands. They had plenty to do that afternoon, anyway, as soon as Grandma was out of the way.

"I'm going over to see Hattie Henderson this afternoon. She phoned this morning and invited me over to tea. Says she came across a bunch of old photograph albums I'd be interested in — people who lived here years ago."

Clancy had a hard time to keep from smiling. Mrs. Henderson was in on the plan, too. Her job was to keep Grandma away from the house all afternoon, so Horace and the boys could set the candles in place.

They worked like beavers, all four of them. It took much longer than they had thought it would, for Horace insisted that each shingle with its four straight-standing candles be placed exactly right along the edge of the roof. Finally they were almost finished.

149

"It's going to look a little bare right here," Horace
called from the roof. "Don't we have any more candles?
We need about — oh, two dozen more, I guess."

The candles were gone, so Clancy raced off to the
hardware store to get some more before Grandma came
back.

Mr. Berry was talking to a customer as Clancy burst
in the store. He was impatient, but he had to wait

politely while the leisurely conversation went on and on.

"Yes sir, things are changing in Mapleton," Mr. Berry said. "Now you take paint. Used to be the only color house paint anybody wanted was white, with green or black for shutters. But now, it's any color in the rainbow, seems like. A fellow out on the edge of town painted his house light green and his neighbor liked it so much he did his house yellow. Next thing I know someone'll come in here and ask for *pink!*"

Mr. Berry laughed his hearty laugh, ha-ha, and the customer laughed, too, and left. Pink, thought Clancy. The girls are going to ice the cupcakes with pink icing. Be nice if Grandma's house was pink, more like a real birthday cake. And the white gingerbread trim would show up swell against pink— He was amazed to hear his own voice saying,

"Two dozen more candles, please, and — do you have any pink house paint?"

Mr. Berry laughed again. He thought Clancy was joking.

"Nope, not in stock. Things haven't got that fancy yet in Mapleton, Clancy. I've got white paint, though, and you could color it up with a tube of red if you're planning to paint your house pink, ha-ha!"

Clancy didn't know what had come over him. Paint Grandma's house pink? Crazy! And yet —

"I'll take it," he said suddenly. "A gallon of white and a tube of red, and please charge it."

151

All the way home with the big can of paint in his bicycle basket, he kept saying to himself, "Of all the wild ideas! Bill and Scudder will think I've come unstrung — and what would Horace say? Pink. Like a real cake. Oh no, I wouldn't dare. Grandma'd have a fit — "

He put the paint in the back shed and carried the candles around to the side yard where the others were waiting for him. He didn't say a word to anyone about his sudden brainstorm.

Mrs. Henderson did her part well. It was almost dusk when Grandma came hurrying home, and she never once glanced up at the roof. She put on her apron and started to wash the salad greens.

"My goodness, I never expected to be so late! I'll have to hurry with supper. Hattie Henderson has photographs of just about everybody who has lived in Mapleton for the last fifty years. Run out to the garden to see if any tomatoes are ripe yet, and bring a handful of parsley, too."

So far so good, thought Clancy, as he went out to the little vegetable plot. With any luck at all Grandma would be rushing around too much tomorrow to notice the lines of candles edging her roof. It would be a real surprise.

Clancy got out the blue and white checked tablecloth and set the round table. As she flew around the kitchen, Grandma asked, "How did you make out all this long

152

afternoon, Clancy? Did you manage to find something to do?"

He grinned. "I was busy, Grandma, just messin' around."

10

CLANCY took off his jacket and loosened his tie a little. Golly, he felt warm, all dressed up. He had worn a polo shirt to the pageant in the afternoon (sitting way in the back of the auditorium so Mrs. Holloway couldn't see him and get rattled) but Grandma had insisted that he be really fixed up for the supper. She had checked on his outfit before she hurried off to the Fire House. Grandma was the honored guest, along with Senator White, and was to sit at a special table with all the important people. She said almost wistfully, "First time in years that I haven't been working in the kitchen at one of these suppers. I sent a bowl of my spiced crab apples, of course. People count on them at a supper, they tell me. But it seems sort of funny not to be taking my apron along to work. I keep thinking it's too bad that none of the Chapmans are taking a real part. It doesn't seem right, somehow."

Clancy chuckled to himself. She'll soon see, he thought happily.

Practically all the women in town were taking their turns at the Fire House. Mrs. Williams and Mrs. Brown were to wait on tables for the first shift of diners, and eat later with the rest of their families. So Clancy and Scudder and Bill were going together. It was all working out beautifully, just as Horace had planned it.

"Mrs. Henderson will be in the kitchen for the second shift, so we'll eat early. Then as soon as we finish we'll all hustle back to Grandma's and get the banner up," Horace had said. By now he was as excited as the boys about winning the prize.

Scudder and Bill came hurrying down Main Street. They were dressed to the teeth, too, in their Sunday suits.

"Hi, Clance. Boy, it's a hot one. But no breeze, thank goodness. Horace said he wouldn't light the candles unless it was really still, and there's not a leaf stirring."

"Come on, let's get there early. The selection is always better at the first tables." Scudder was an expert where food was concerned.

They walked along, not fast — it was too hot to hurry — but not wasting any time, either. Scudder remarked, "It sure has been a nice day. The parade and the band concert this afternon were swell, and even the pageant wasn't too bad."

The other two agreed. Clancy said, "As long as we weren't up there hopping around, it was pretty good. I really liked it, especially where the pioneers built the log cabin and Georgie let the log fall."

They scooted in and out of the groups of strolling townspeople, and when the doors opened promptly at five, the Tigers were first in line. They chose seats near the door so they could leave quickly when they finished.

"Get a whiff, fellows," whispered Scudder ecstatically. "Did you ever smell anything so good?"

The Fire House was soon full. Clancy could see Grandma at the other end of the room, saying something to Senator White that made that worthy gentleman roar with laughter. Clancy was pleased that Grandma was enjoying herself. He glowed inside when he thought of the surprise she was going to get later in the evening.

The big Fire House was full of noise, of talking and laughing and the clink of dishes as they were passed up and down the long tables. Every lady in town had loaned at least one cut-glass bowl or hand-painted plate. There were flowers on the tables and on the ladies' best summer hats. There was color for the eyes and cheerful noise for the ears and wonderful smells to tickle the nose. It was a most satisfying event.

The Tigers didn't say much. They were too busy eating. At last even Scudder couldn't hold another bite. He looked longingly at a magnificent coconut cake that his mother was cutting and shook his head.

"I've sampled everything else," he murmured sadly, "but I'll have to pass that up."

"I don't see why, when you've only tried three kinds of pie, and strawberry shortcake besides." Bill laughed, but he didn't take any cake either.

"I don't know if I'd dare get up on the roof now," groaned Clancy. "I'd break it down. I hope we walk off some of this stuffed feeling on our way to Grandma's."

As they left the Fire House, Horace hurried out the back door and called to them.

"There's been a slight hitch in our plans," he told them. "The ladies have latched onto me for kitchen duty — seems they're short of men to carry the heavy trays — so I can't get away right now. Can you get the banner up alone?" he asked anxiously.

"Nothing to it," the boys assured him. "We'll manage fine."

"Now mind you, just the banner. Don't dare do any of the candle-lighting without me. I'll be along as soon as I can get away."

They had no problem at all with the banner. Horace had screwed big hooks into the siding of the house. It was easy to hang the long banner over the hooks and arrange it neatly so the lettering showed plainly, Happy Birthday Mapleton 1722–1922.

There was no need to be secretive. Not a soul passed as they worked. Everyone in town was at the Fire House or next door in the Town Hall where the orchestra was playing.

It was all ready in a few minutes. There was nothing to do then but sit on the steps and wait for Horace. Clancy kept going inside to check the time on the cuckoo clock in the kitchen.

"Only six-fifteen," he reported dismally. "Mr. Hadley said the judging wouldn't begin until at least seven forty-five, and we're the last place on the list. It's going to be a l-o-o-ong wait."

"Can't we do something more, some little thing that would make it look better?" Scudder wanted action.

"Come on, Clancy, think of something sensational."

"I've already had an idea," said Clancy slowly, "but maybe it's too sensational."

The boys whistled when Clancy told them about the pink paint, and agreed that it was sensational — but what would Grandma say?

"Maybe nothing if we win the prize. Or maybe she'll skin us alive. It's a chance we'll have to take," said Clancy cheerfully. He was beginning to think that his brainstorm hadn't been so bad, after all. Scudder was convinced, too. He rolled up his sleeves, all ready to get to work. Bill thought it over, and then he grinned and nodded like a cheerful owl.

"We can do it in time, can't we? All we'd need to paint is the front of the house, and it's not very big."

"The color has to be mixed. I'll do that and you two scout around for brushes."

They were gaining momentum now — the plan was rolling. Clancy stirred and stirred until the thick white paint was smooth. Then he squeezed out a little of the red paint Mr. Berry had sold him. He stirred and stirred some more. He watched breathlessly, but nothing happened. The paint seemed about as white as before, so he added a little more red, and followed that with more stirring. A faint pink tint showed but it was so pale that it would seem white under the street light.

Desperately, Clancy squeezed out the rest of the paint, rolling up the tube to get out the last little bit.

159

He stirred again, round and round, and all of a sudden the gallon of paint turned a decided pink, darker and darker as he mixed it. It was the luscious bright color of strawberries crushed in cream.

"Wow!" breathed Clancy. "We've got us a real pink!"

Bill and Scudder hurried back with the brushes they had found in Brown's shed. Clancy divided the paint into smaller cans, and got out the tall ladder and Grandma's kitchen step ladder. One of them could work standing on a regular chair for the lower parts.

"This won't take long," said Scudder briskly as he started up the ladder. "The front of the house is mostly windows, anyway." He unhooked the banner and Clancy and Bill rolled it up and put it inside the front door.

"Wait a minute," Bill remembered. "We're all dressed up. I know what my mother will say if I get paint on my best suit."

Nothing stopped Scudder for long. Holding on to the ladder and the paint can with one hand, he loosened his belt. He stepped out of his best trousers with some difficulty while the others watched anxiously from below.

"Here," he said jauntily, as he dropped the trousers down to Clancy. "Put 'em inside with my jacket, will you? BVDs are cooler, anyway, and nobody is going to see us working in our underwear."

160

So the three painters, stripped to their underwear, started to work. As he slapped the first brushful on the white house Bill gasped. "This sure is a loud pink, Clancy. Did you have to make it so bright?"

It was bright, even brighter than it had looked in the

can. Clancy stared at the pink patch in horror. He was sure that he had made a terrible mistake, but they had gone too far now to turn back. He had no more white paint to add.

"I must have rocks in my head," said Clancy miserably. "I don't know what I was thinking of, to get us in a mess like this." But the three wide pink swatches were on the house now, and there wasn't much they could do about it.

"It would look like measles if we stopped," said Bill doubtfully. "I guess we'll have to finish it up. But don't feel bad, Clancy, you didn't make the mistake all alone. We agreed."

"Never mind, Clance, it'll be an eye-catcher, all right, and when it dries we can paint the whole front white again." Scudder tried to be consoling, but his effort wasn't very convincing.

They went to work, but there was no heart in their effort. Now that their enthusiasm for the project had waned, the small house front seemed very large indeed. They worked away doggedly, with only the slap of the brushes punctuating the silence. From down the street came the lively sound of the orchestra playing away in the Town Hall basement, but it did nothing to cheer them up. It was almost dark when they finished. Scudder came down from the ladder, and all three stepped back to see how it looked.

"It's streaky. I guess I didn't stir it enough."

"It sure won't stand the bright light of day," agreed Bill, "but maybe when the lights come on — "

It was just then eight o'clock, and as always in the summer the street lights were turned on.

"Wowee!" yelled Scudder. "Look at that!"

Under the soft glow of the street lamp, the little house shone. It was a bright pink all right, a cheerful smiling color. The fancy white gingerbread that edged the roof and windows and porch pillars stood out clear and clean against the pink. There was no doubt about it, Grandma's house was an eyecatcher!

"It really looks good enough to eat," said Scudder, slightly awed by what they had accomplished. "Like strawberry shortcake — "

"Or birthday cake. Hurry, let's get the banner back up again. We haven't much more time."

They raced to hang up the banner, working as fast as they could, yet careful not to get any pink paint on the white cloth. They put away the ladders and the paint cans, and tried to clean their very painty hands. They were just struggling into their trousers when Horace hurried up the street. He stopped short when he saw the house. The Tigers waited fearfully to hear what he would say.

For a while it looked as if the shock of the pink house had stricken him dumb. When he did speak, the words came out all mixed up, sort of as if he were gargling. Finally he asked, "Does — does G-grandma know about th-this?" The Tigers shook their heads.

"Well, I sure hope she likes it. But if she doesn't, I'll tell her she's getting old. I think this place looks cute as a button, and I'll stick with you even if she cuts off our heads and serves us with sauerkraut."

Now their spirits soared. If Horace liked it and they liked it — who knows? Maybe the judges would like it, too. They tried not to think about what Grandma might say.

Dulcy, Pat, Lou-Ann, Dodie and Emily came rushing down the street from the Williams house, all loaded with baskets of cupcakes.

"The judging is almost over, they're on Park Street already!" the girls shouted, and then stood open-mouthed as they caught sight of the house. "Ooooooooooh, it's wonderful! It just matches the icing on the cupcakes!"

"Park Street!" Horace sprang into action. "Time to start lighting the candles."

He climbed up from the back of the house, because of the wet paint, and went along the edge of the roof, lighting each candle with a long taper. At first the candles sputtered and flickered, and their light was dim and uncertain. Then, just as the Mayor's big touring car turned the corner into Main Street, the flames straightened and burned with a steady glow. The whole house appeared to leap into radiance.

The Tigers stood on the sidewalk, transfixed, until

Horace hissed, "Get inside, you chowderheads! You'll spoil the effect."

Horace stayed on the roof, crouched out of sight behind the cupola, in case of fire. The Tigers dashed in the door only seconds before the cavalcade of cars stopped out in front. They were in the darkened parlor, noses pressed against the front window. They watched eagerly as the judges stared. They couldn't see Grandma, hidden behind the Senator's bulk.

"Now," said Clancy, giving the signal to Dulcy. The girls started out the front door with their baskets of cupcakes. It seemed too quiet outside, not a bit gay or festive. There was a big crowd of people but nobody was cheering or clapping or anything. They just stood and looked, hushed. In the silence, Lou-Ann suddenly began to sing. Her voice was small and piping, all alone. Then Dulcy and Pat joined in, and Emily and Dodie, and then the crowd began to sing, too. Even Senator White was roaring at the top of his lungs, "Happy Birthday, dear Mapleton, Happy Birthday to you!"

"Thank heavens for the girls," said Scudder, and neither Bill or Clancy thought it was an unusual thing to hear him say.

Then everything was a wonderful, joyous madhouse. The girls passed out the cupcakes, and made trip after trip back to the house for more. The Senator was standing up in the back seat of the Mayor's open car, trying to make a speech, but nobody listened. Mr. Jones was there, eating cupcakes and cheering between bites. The people of Mapleton clapped and hollered, and as Grandma said afterwards, proud as a peacock, "made regular fools of themselves."

There was no doubt about who had won the prize. People began to shout, "Grandma! Grandma! We want Grandma Chapman!" The Senator made her stand up on the seat beside him.

Everybody quieted down as Grandma said in her thin little old voice, "I didn't have one thing to do with this! In fact, if I'd been asked I'd have probably said no. But I've got a pretty good idea who did do it. Dulcy, get those Tigers out here to take a bow."

The Tigers came out, sheepish, flushed with triumph, and considerably paint-stained. Then they called Horace down from the roof, and the girls were gathered together, and the photographer from the *Times-Chronicle* lined all nine of them up on the porch and took their picture. It was a glorious Fourth of July.

When at long last it was all over, Grandma slipped out of her best shoes and sank down in her rocker.

"Run along to the fireworks, kids," she said happily, wearily. "I'm going to sit right here on the porch and watch the high ones above the trees."

Clancy was the last to leave. As he sat beside her she rumpled his red hair lovingly.

"Don't stay up too late, Clancy, because tomorrow morning early the Tigers are going to paint the rest of this house pink. You young fellows can do the low work, but *I* intend to paint the cupola."